MW01610158

Advance Praise

"**Fate Date** is good reading. The plot thickens. Romance, friendship, betrayal. Curiouser and curiouser. What's next?" - **Anne Juhasz**

"**Fate Date** is a quick and easy read. Author Mitch Phillis' style reminds me of Hemingway's. Short and straight-forward. I definitely want to read more about Barb and Mr. Lofland!" - **Tatiana Roberts**

"Plot details such as DARPA's involvement and the fate algorithm (a big Sci-Fi feel) is campy, similar to a typical *Twilight Zone*. I'd go further to say that the whole **F8D8** series will be at home in a collection of *Twilight Zone* screenplays." - **Reid G. FitzGerald**

The Author

Mitch Phillis is an emerging storyteller who grew up with an imagination that flowed naturally and quietly. On the floor with pencil and paper, drawing was his earliest creative expression. From there, his interest grew all the way to an art degree from Mercyhurst University. Neither reading or writing ever came as easily. In his words... "Ironically, I could barely *read* until the fourth grade, so writing a book felt like an impossibility. Until now. A creative idea has manifested itself. *Fate Date* has found its way into this, my first book. I hope you enjoy it!"

Uncle Mitch with his youngest fan

To my friends and family who supported me in stepping outside my comfort zone, and to my writing coach Steve FitzGerald (OhioWritingCoach.com) who without, I would have never been able to have the confidence to follow through on writing this book. -- **Mitch Phillis**

For updates on the Fate Date series, follow Mitch on Twitter @FateDateBook or visit his website at FateDateBook.com

FATE DATE

THE F8D8 FILES

Mitch Phillis

Spring 1919

THE GREYHOUND BUS SLOWED to a stop to drop off its only passenger destined for the small town. The driver proudly called out, "Beautiful downtown Salem, Ohio. It's 8:10 a.m. Right on time! Please watch your step, Miss."

Carrying her travel bag and purse, Barbara McFadden carefully steps onto the curb near the corner of State Street and Broadway Avenue. As the bus pulls away, it reveals that the two streets meet like a capital T. Looking in all three directions -- to her left and right, and straight ahead -- she can see that Salem's downtown storefronts only go a block or two each way.

The bus driver had told her there was a secretarial opening at the *Farm & Dairy* newspaper.

"The publisher himself told me they needed a typist ASAP."

A newsboy on the opposite corner raises his arm, paper in hand, and calls out to her.

"Miss, would you like the latest paper?"

He doesn't wait for her to answer before he crosses the street to where she's standing.

She smiles at him, then answers, "Oh, I'm sorry. I don't have time to read it. But thank you very much for asking me."

"Sure lady!" he replies in a chipper voice.

"By the way, can you point me in the direction of the *Farm & Dairy* newspaper's office?"

"You bet I can. It's that way, all the way down East State. It's the last storefront on that side," he says, pointing with the paper. "I even know the address number. Do you want it?"

Again, he doesn't wait for her to answer.

"185. It's 185 East State Street. My name is Joe. I'm the newspaper's best salesman!" he adds without hesitating.

"Well Joe, I'm not the least bit surprised that you are the best! Thank you for the address."

"You're welcome, lady. If you come back this way, maybe get a paper. I mean if I have any left. If I don't, then you won't see me."

He returns to his usual spot across the street.

After taking in the scenery of a waking downtown -- and meeting Joe -- she closes her eyes for a few seconds and enjoys the sunny warmth on her face.

She takes in a deep breath, and as she exhales, smiles. She opens her eyes then waves to the paperboy. Joe waves back.

She's feeling confident that she's in the right place at the right time. She's excited, nervous and motivated all at once. An optimist by nature, she's also a realist and usually prepared for whatever outcomes could come her way. She's feeling fearless.

State and Broadway are her starting point, and she's ready to take on the day.

The bank across the corner has a large copper clock with two faces that display the time to pedestrians walking from any direction. The small hand is on the eight, the large one near the three. Right on time, she amusingly recalls. She doesn't have an appointment or anywhere she must be, at any particular time. Still, her first goal today is to get an interview at the *Farm & Dairy*.

Barbara believes she can handle just about any job, but she also knows that the options in Salem will be limited. She would like to find a job at the hospital, but those are likely the better jobs in town. She'll need to get to know the locals and get established. In the meantime, she'll take a job typing.

"To 185," she affirms to herself, heading down East State.

She passes a busy diner, a hardware, then a small dress shop. The next storefront is vacant, and she can't help give herself a quick once-over in the window's reflection.

Her light-brown hair is swooped to one side and pinned up, curls flowing down, nearly touching her shoulders. Her floral-patterned dress, which she sewed, peeks out from the bottom of her long, dark green peacoat that she has belted closed. Her short-heeled tan shoes finish her outfit.

Growing up, others had often called her a "cute girl." More recently, she had become a "beautiful young woman." But she never thought of herself as either, and she was certainly not a princess, as some who were jealous called her. She has always -- and very proudly -- considered herself more of a worker bee. An excellent worker.

She has a big contagious smile and a thinner bridged nose, with soft hazel eyes. She doesn't know it, but it's her eyes that attract the most attention when people first meet her. They have a gentle glimmer that makes her non-threatening and inviting. You feel that she's a friendly and compassionate person. Combined with her half-crooked and relatable smile, she could probably have her own way and get away with anything -- this she *does* know.

She's dressed in her best and the window's reflection feels good to her. She tugs on her coat's knotted belt, then turns and crosses to the other side of State.

She stops on the sidewalk in front of the last storefront and looks up at the modest, hanging *Farm & Dairy* sign. Inside the window, there's a white cardboard sign, professionally printed... Help Wanted: Assistant Secretary.

She walks in the door and greets the woman at the front desk, "Hello, I'm Barbara McFadden and I'm here to enquire about the assistant secretary position."

"Oh, terrific," she enthusiastically responds.

After introducing herself, Dee, the long-time office manager and personal secretary to the publisher asks her only one interview question.

"Do you know how to use a typewriter, Barbara?"

"Yes ma'am. In fact, I was the fastest typist in my class. And please, my friends call me Barb."

Maybe it was her air of confidence or how well she presented herself. Or maybe it was purely out of the paper's need. It was probably all of the above that prompted Dee to offer her the job on the spot.

After Barb agrees to the fair starting wage that comes with the position, Dee has a second question for her.

"Can you start right now? I know this is an unusual request, but we are swamped and falling too far behind. We really have to get caught up with renewing subscribers and invoicing our advertisers."

Knowing help has finally arrived, Dee is clearly relieved, yet fully disclosing of everything needing attention.

"Plus, there's composing, typing and mailing correspondence. Not to mention, Mr. Darling's various errands. His laundry is beginning to pile up, too. The last gal we had went and eloped with her boyfriend, and left the job without giving us an iota of notice."

As if to underscore the urgency of her request, two telephones start ringing.

Barb adds sympathy to her respect for Dee.

"Yes, I can start right now. I'll get that phone and take a message while you answer the one on your desk."

A few minutes later, after things have calmed, the *Farm & Dairy*'s owner rolls in the front door. Wayne T. Darling has just returned from vacation but is freshly shaven, wearing a fedora and, as usual, he's in a nice suit and tie. In one hand, he holds an unlit cigar. In the other, his *Journal of Commerce* newspaper.

"Good morning, Dee."

"Good morning, Mr. Darling."

He then turns to Barb and says, "Young lady, with that travel bag, are you coming or going?"

"Actually, I just arrived in Salem this morning. And I'm your new assistant secretary."

Dee interjects, "This is Barbara McFadden, and she's agreed to start work today.

Barbara is extremely qualified for our secretarial position, especially in typing."

"That's excellent, Dee! Is it Mrs. or Miss McFadden, and do you have lodging?"

"No, I haven't looked for a rental yet. I needed to find a job first! And it's Miss."

He begins searching through his suit coat pockets and finally pulls out a rubber-banded bunch of business cards. He shuffles through them until he finds one calling card in particular, which he then hands to her.

"The Lofland House. It's a very respectable boarding house. In fact, the proprietor is one of our many loyal advertisers. Tell him I said he must give you the *Farm & Dairy* family rate... at least until you get your first weekly paycheck!"

He chuckles at his own wit, while the ladies smile.

Chapter 2

DR. DANIEL CARR HAS been delivering babies for nearly four decades. He has always had a deep passion for lowering infantile death rates and has dedicated his life to studying and examining mothers and their newborns.

He lives for his work. He lost the love of his life many years ago and has solely focused on his work ever since. He's neurotic, a little socially awkward most of the time, but he's an excellent doctor and researcher.

His studies have elevated him to the forefront of placenta research, and he is acclaimed as one of the best in the field. He has always believed that the placenta contains the key to life and holds a special characteristic in carrying both the mother's and fetus' DNA.

Dr. Carr is one of the founding physicians who raised funds to build the Salem City Hospital. He had great influence in its planning, because he was awarded a grant as well as the newest medical technology available from the federal government. As a result, he has a research laboratory with its own private office in the hospital's basement.

For the federal funding, he's always been expected to treat all information specific to his research as classified material. But very quickly, he found it not only annoying but impractical and inefficient. Rather than keeping the classified files in the basement and having to continually update them separately, he decided he could kill two birds with one stone. So, he developed a better system which allows him to keep all the information in one file by using a secret code to protect the classified information. This allows him to work upstairs with classified information in hand, without the security risk.

Hi research project has been receiving funding for for nearly five years. He felt guilty about this during the war and even penned a letter to the head of the agency, to offer back his funding until the war was over. In spite of his never receiving a response, his funding continued without interruption.

Just a few months ago, the war was won. He wrote another letter, this time requesting additional help for his research in the form of a mathematician. Again, there was no response to his request.

The elevator arrives and opens on the first floor.

Surprised, Sally says, "Hi Doc! The receptionist asked me to tell you there's someone in the lobby for you. I was on my way to let you know."

"Did you see who it is?"

"No, I didn't. She just said a Mr. Newman is waiting and asked me to let you know." She shrugs.

"Thank you, Sally."

Dr. Carr exits the elevator and rounds the corner to the reception desk, where he sees one person waiting. He looks to the receptionist who nods toward the lone visitor. The gentleman is dressed in a suit and tie, wearing glasses, and is holding a briefcase.

"Hello, I'm Dr. Daniel Carr. How may I help you?" he offers, as they shake hands.

"Hello sir, I'm Matthew Newman and I've been sent by the agency that funds your research."

"Yes sir, yes sir, of course. Right this way," he says, trying to hide his surprise.

The elevator door closes behind them. Dr. Carr's mind is racing. He fears his funding may be finished.

Newman is tall, or at least seems that way to the average-height doctor. He has darker blonde hair combed across, and a clean-cut look. He looks to be all business, but has a kind face. He's intimidating, but this may be due to his being equally quiet.

Fortunately, it's a short ride to the basement -- only one floor -- so their silence goes unnoticed.

In the basement, they walk down the hall to his laboratory office. Dr. Carr uses a key to unlock the steel double doors. Then he flips to a second key on his ring and opens the interior door to his office.

"Mr. Newman, please have a seat."

"Thank you, Dr. Carr."

The doctor waits for him to continue. But he doesn't. The silence prompts him to speak again, nervously and rapidly.

"I wasn't sure my letters were being received. I've been doing great work. I also have been managing the project funding very efficiently. I just wasn't sure what or how to, or who I should be speaking with."

"Were you not expecting me?" Newman asks.

"Oh I was, I was. I just didn't know when," the doctor pretended. "I really do have a lot to share with you."

"Sir, I think there's some confusion. I'm the mathematician you requested."

"Right, right. Of course. I didn't know the agency granted my request. This is very good."

"Yes sir, but I'll be completely honest. I really don't know anything about the nature and status of your research. I was just promoted after the war and transferred to another agency, then I was given instructions re-assigning me to come here," the young man explains.

"Well, what agency sent you? Do you have a supervisor?" the relieved doctor asks.

"It was Director Yardley who promoted and transferred me to DARPA. He said someone from DARPA would be in touch shortly, to supervise our work. He didn't know who."

"I'm not familiar with DARPA. What is it?"

"I'm sorry. I should have explained first. It's brand-new federal agency. The Department of Advanced Research Projects and Analysis. I hope to learn more about its funding and mission soon. DARPA's name hasn't been officially approved yet, but in my instructions, I'm to start using it internally, and externally when on field assignments."

"Oh. Well, let me explain why I need your help. I've been collecting every form of data I can from each mother, newborn and placenta for twenty years. The advanced technology the government granted my research has allowed me to begin forming correlations between these three, all the way down to their respective cells. There is a code here. There is a key here. Once we put it all together in the right equation, we may be able to eliminate infants deaths altogether. This is extremely important work."

"Yes, it certainly is, Dr. Carr. I look forward to helping. How would you like me to get started?"

Chapter 3

AFTER HER FIRST DAY at work, Barb walks past the paperboy's corner. *He must have sold out. Good for Joe*, she thinks.

Following directions Dee wrote down for her, she continues to the corner of South Lincoln and Franklin, only a couple blocks south of downtown.

The hard-to-miss wooden sign stands prominently in the front yard with its engraved, script-like letters: *The Lofland Boarding House*. Hanging below it, a smaller sign announces VACANCY in stenciled, block letters.

The large house sits back from the shaded side-walked corner. It's painted a light blue with white trim, topped by a taller main roof of slate. White classical columns support the roofs of its wrap-around porch and drive-up portico.

The driveway curves around the entire house and connects both streets of the intersection. A holly hedgerow extends from both ends of the driveway, running along both sidewalks.

On the Lincoln side, the evergreen hedge breaks to reveal thick Berea sandstone steps leading to the front yard's sidewalk. As Barb walks toward the front porch, the house seems to grow larger.

Tall bushes around the porch make seeing onto it impossible. But as she ascends the porch's light-gray stone steps, she sees an old man rising from one of several rocking chairs.

His beard is almost pure white. Some strands of gray and white hair are combed across the top of his head.

As if waiting for her arrival, he has a ready smile and a friendly greeting for her.

"Welcome to The Lofland House. I'm Keith Lofland and I'm the owner."

"It's nice to meet you. I'm Barbara McFadden. Your sign says that you have a room available."

"Yes. How long do you plan to stay?"

Barb explains how she's new to town and has already started her job at the *Farm & Dairy*.

"Right! Wayne gave me a ring and said you'd be coming. He also told me that I'd better give you a family discount on the rent!"

Barb laughs. "Already? His word must travel fast!"

"Most of the time it does," he says. "Now, let me show your around inside."

He leads her to the heavy, hand-carved front door.

"What a beautiful entrance. It's so grand," she says.

The door's woodwork is elaborate. The threshold, floor and trim are all a rich mahogany brown.

"The porch and entrance are clearly well-crafted. And I love these beveled glass panes in this door. One can just tell that your house was built with an attention to detail, and to be around for an exceptionally long time."

Mr. Lofland beams. "Thank you for noticing the details. She has good bones. But I still need to work on her every day, so she stays looking good as she does. You could say I'm married to this house. She's my labor of love!"

From the entryway, they step into the foyer where she can't help but notice the floral Turkish wool rug covering most of the floor.

"This carpeting is so lovely," she says.

"My family has always taken a lot of pride in the home's furnishing," he comments.

He continues, recalling some early history of the home's appointments, but Barb is only half listening. Instead, she's taking in every ornate detail on her own.

The first two rooms have large openings without doors. The room to the left is a reading or smoking room. It's carpeted, and has leather couches and chairs. Built-in bookcases are on both sides of a large, brick fireplace.

To the right is a large parlor. She imagines it filled with a gathering of fancy, party guests sipping champagne. A larger fireplace is centered on the far wall, with a gold-framed mirror above it.

The gathering room flows into the dining room, separated by wooden and glass pocket-doors that slide back into the walls. On this sunny day, the room has several windows that illuminate it. A window seat winds around a corner of the room, travels underneath several sills, and abuts a bookcase on the wall, next to the pocket doors.

Mounted on the room's ceiling, above the large dining table, is an eight-armed, four-tiered crystal and brass chandelier. The sunlight seems to dance within its hand-cut lead crystal facets.

Connecting the dining room to the kitchen is a swinging door. Painted gray, it has engraved brass push and kick plates. It has a round, portal window to warn of traffic coming to or from either room.

Mr. Lofland's detailed history lesson continues, despite a loud clanking noise coming from the next room. They work their way around the dining table. Barb's focus turns to the commotion coming from the kitchen. Suddenly, the swing door bursts open.

A young woman kicks through the door, drops and plate of food on the table then turns to Mr. Lofland.

"Fourteen hours straight. I think Doc is trying to kill me, Keith!"

She appears to be in her early-20s and, by her manner, maybe rough around the edges. She looks tired and she's definitely on the edge. She's wearing a nurse's uniform, a long white skirt with a white button-up top.

Her shoulder-length dark hair, which appears to have been pinned up all day -- probably under a white bonnet -- is messily fallen.

"Miss McFadden, this is Sally. Sally is my longest boarder. I just try to stay out of her way," he jokes.

"You *better* stay out of my way!" she seriously shoots back at him, as she takes a seat at the table.

She's a tough one, thinks Barb.

"Miss McFadden might be moving in," he explains to Sally.

"Sally, please call me Barb."

After she forks in a few more bites of food, she looks up at Barb.

"So maybe I'll see you around," she muffles while chewing chicken.

"Not if she sees you first!" Mr. Lofland jokes once more. Sally ignores him.

"Maybe. It's nice to meet you, Sally," Barb offers.

"Yeah, same," she muffles through her food-filled mouth. "I gotta run. I don't want to be late."

Sally stands up and takes her plate into the kitchen. Its backdoor slamming signals her departure. And a return to the business at hand.

"Mr. Lofland, may I see the available room? And what is its rent on a monthly basis?"

He explains that the four-dollar rent includes use of a shared bathing room and a daily dinner served served at six o'clock. As they move through the swing door, she notices a small bell with a pull string, mounted on the dining room side of the doorway's trim.

"Is this a dinner bell?"

"You guessed it. But I never ring it. Just don't forget that I have dinner served hot and ready right at six. If you're late and your food is cold, don't come complaining to me!" he warns, in good humor.

The kitchen cabinets are dark wood, matching the rest of the downstairs trim. Some of the cabinets have beveled glass fronts, elegant enough to display fine china. Overall, the kitchens is clean and orderly, she notes.

"Let me show you the room. It's on the second floor."

After passing through another kitchen doorway, he points out a tiny lavatory tucked under the main staircase. The wide stairs are adorned with elaborately crafted handrails that run up about a dozen steps to a landing. On it, against the exterior wall, is a built-in seat with a very tall window lighting the stairs and landing.

They continue up another dozens steps to the second floor. Off its landing is a door that opens to reveal a twisting stairway. He points up the stairs and says, "Men stay on the third floor. No reason to go up there. This floor is for women."

He closes the door and pivots to survey the wide common area where they are standing. There are two doors on his right side, and three on his left. An open door straight ahead reveals the bathing room. He leads her to a closed door on the left side of the hall.

"This here is Sally's room. She's sometime and handful." The he quickly adds, "But she means well and like I said, she's been here the longest. Basically, she came with the place when we changed it from an orphanage into a boarding house."

"Really?"

"Yes. At the time, she was of age so that she could just stay in place, and she got herself a job so she could pay the rent. She never pays on time, but that's another story. Hopefully, you gals will get along okay."

"I'm sure we could," Barb politely says.

He continues with the tour, next leading her to the large, shared bathroom.

"Each room has its own sink with running water, but you share this room for bathing. This is just for you women to use."

White tiles cover the floor and, looking in, a clawfoot tub sits on the left. For showering, above the tub is a pulled-back curtain that can be swung around it. Two copper waterlines sprout from the floor and meet just above the tub edge, behind three small knobs. One line continues toward the ceiling where it holds a shower head shaped like a blooming sunflower. To the right, a white porcelain toilet sits next to a marble sink with a matching mirror.

"It's very nice, Mr. Lofland."

"Thank you. Now, you want to see your room? It's this door over here."

He opens the door directly across from Sally's room. They walk in and he goes over to the window and pulls open the drapes.

Sun floods the room and highlights the canopy bed. This isn't some hole-in-the-wall neglected rooming house.

The room is much more than what Barb was expecting.

"My goodness, the canopy bed is so beautiful and this room is so large."

"Like I said, the house used to be an orphanage. Most of the rooms had several beds in 'em. This room had girls' bunk beds in those two corners, and baby cribs on this end."

Barb likes the room.

She likes Mr. Lofland.

She likes the price.

"I'll take it!"

Chapter 4

BARB STANDS UP FROM her desk as Mr. Darling enters the office. He first greets his long-time secretary, "Morning, Dee."

"Good morning, sir."

Flashing a look at Barb, he jokingly asks Dee, "And how is the new girl doing?"

"Quite well. She types more than 80 words per minute. Without a single mistake!"

"Well, I'll be! That's pretty darn good, Miss Barb!" he says, turning to her.

"Thank you, Mr. Darling."

"At the end of the day, please come up to my office so I can learn a little more about you," he instructed.

"Certainly, sir!"

After checking with Dee to get his messages and mail, he proceeds upstairs.

This being the start of Barb's second day, she hasn't exactly been overwhelmed by her initial assignments. The tasks she was asked to help with were quite simple and easy for her.

She accepts that office duties and errands will never be exciting. They simply just need to be done. At the same time, it's in Barb's nature to want to do any assignment as best as it can be done. She likes to impress, no matter what the task is.

Maybe the best example was her first trip to Ray's Cleaners...

"Hello? I have Mr. Darling's shirts
to be laundered and pressed,"
she announces upon entering.
She places them on the counter,
then leans to her left to try to
see around the carousel of clean
clothes on new wire hangers.

A man yells from the back, "Okay!

I will take care of them. You can leave them on the counter. Medium starch as usual?"

"Yes, please. Also, I need to ask you about cleaning his winter coat. Is wool going to be a problem for you?"

A short, older gentleman emerges from around the other side of the carousel.

"You must be new," he quips.

"Yes sir. I'm Barbara McFadden and I'm Dee's new assistant secretary."

"Very good. I'm Ray. And yes, we clean wool. I've personally been handling Mr. Darling's dry cleaning as long as I've been in business."

"Oh swell, Ray... maybe you can help me out. With this being my

first errand, I would really like
to make a good impression. What
kind of discount do you normally
extend to Mr. Darling?"

Surprised, he gazed up from
tagging the stack of shirts, and
could only muster, "A discount?"

She responded with a hopeful
smile.

Ray nodded with a look of
understanding and said, "Okay,
I'll drop the price a nickel."

To which, Barb offered her biggest
smile, and her eyes opened a little
wider after an extra blink.

"Sir, please, could you do a little
better?"

"Fine, a dime," he offered. A bit
embarrassed, he thought it smart
to add, "Yes, a dime is better for
him! I've been meaning to start

*discounting Mr. Darling anyway.
Just been so busy. I'll call and
tell him about his discount. And
I'll be sure to give you credit for
reminding me, Miss McFadden."*

*"Well, thank you so very much,
Ray!" she replied, as she twisted to
leave. The bottom of her long dress
swooped around with her turn.
She felt accomplished, finding a
way to make a rather boring task
both fun and rewarding.*

Though Barb could win a race on her
typewriter, her first workday was going by
slowly. Finally, it was quitting time.

Not forgetting Mr. Darling's invitation, she
walks up the stairs to his office. Before she
can give his open door a knock, he sees her
and erupts with an amused bellow.

"Ha haaa! You shook Ray down! I cannot believe it. Well done, Miss Barb, well done! Come in and please have a seat."

His large desk and the surrounding tables are covered with stacks of papers, typesetting tools and metal letterpress blocks. Dark wooden shelves line two walls, nearly every inch filled with books and knickknacks.

The ashtray on the corner of his desk holds a smoked-out cigar, giving the room a lingering charred smell. The windows behind him look down onto State. They back-light him, making him a nearly opaque silhouette of himself.

Barb sits in one of the sturdy wooden chairs in front of his desk. She folds her hands in her lap and smiles at him.

"I already like you, Miss McFadden. I like your style."

"Thank you, Mr. Darling."

"Is Dee treating you well?"

"Yes sir, she is very professional, hard-working and nice."

"You have given me an idea."

Mr. Darling is an intuitive businessman, smart enough to break the mold when he feels it's the profitable thing to do. Although the newspaper has never had a woman writer, he has the instant idea that she can give the paper an extra something. He crafts his idea out loud to her.

"I would like you to write a weekly column, something the farm wives might enjoy." To entice her, he adds, "You would be the *Farm & Dairy*'s very first woman columnist!"

Barb's thoughts pause. She doesn't consider herself a writer. But she likes the idea of breaking tradition, of breaking ground. Plus, this would give her a voice in the community. It would also fill the void she feels from just typing and running mindless errands.

"Do you think you can handle this assignment?"

"Yes, I think I can. I can come up with something for the women. Thank you for the opportunity, Mr. Darling!"

"Excellent! May we call you *Miss Barb*?"

"Why, of course."

"Great, it's a terrific title for your new column!"

Chapter 5

BARB LIKES HER ROOM at the Lofland House. She feels as comfortable as she's ever felt in a new place. Sitting on the edge of her bed, she falls back, opening her arms out wide. A million thoughts are moving through her mind, but not any one specific. It's as if her brain is searching for the first worry or a problem to solve next.

Two loud, quick knocks on her door startle her. She pops up quickly to answer. It's Sally.

"Hey, are you getting in the shower soon or can I get in first? I feel like I've got gunk all over me."

Sally is already wrapped in a bath towel, clearly wanting to get into the shower as soon as possible.

"No, I've already showered. It's all yours, Sally," Barb says cheerfully, though a bit surprised and pleased that Sally has bothered to ask.

"You know there are not too many ladies who make their way through here. It's kind of refreshing for once," explains Sally, as she walks toward the washroom. "Thanks!" she yips, before swinging the door closed.

What a character, Barb thinks as she closes her door. Nonetheless, she's pleased to have Sally, another woman, in the house – it makes it feel like she isn't alone.

The first impression she had of Sally in the dining room was that she was a wild one, a lone wolf type who wasn't interested in getting along. Someone who would rather get by on her own.

Sally definitely had an independent and aggressive attitude earlier, but Barb didn't think that was necessarily a bad thing – at times, she has a similar disposition.

Also, Sally could be her *in*. Before meeting her, Barb was thinking it would be helpful to know someone at the hospital, to get a job there. She and Sally may not become best friends, but there could be some ways where they could help each other.

She tucks herself into bed, but now she has something else on her mind. What is she going to write about in her first column? What could she write about that would be acceptable to Mr. Darling? She wants to write something that will give women reading it a sense of entertainment and hope, something that is progressive but not offensive. She wants to push the envelope but knows she could be in danger of losing the privilege. Maybe just play it safe the first few columns?

I know. Tomorrow, I'll ask Sally what she thinks I should write about. She might know better.

The next morning, after ironing a new blouse she bought, Barb decides Sally should be awake by now and in her room.

Tap, tap, tap. She lightly knocks on Sally's door.

"What?!" Sally yells from inside her room.

"It's Barb."

Sally swings her door open, sporting a look as if confused at why she's being disturbed.

"Sally, I'd appreciate your opinion on what I should write about in my first article for the *Farm & Dairy*."

"I don't give opinions," she answers. She begins closing her door.

Barb stops the door with her foot.

"What are you doing?!"

"Please Sally, I just need your perspective. Just give me a few minutes."

"I don't need you bothering me. Don't you get that?!?"

"No ma'am, I don't get that. I get that you're tough and independent. So am I, and I think we're a lot alike. That's why we should be helping each other, instead of whatever this is. We'll never progress as women if we're fighting each other. We need to stand together and support each other. Then we can all move forward!"

"Okay, so write about that then!" Sally bluntly replies. After a few seconds of awkward silence, she continues.

"Write about how it's such bull crap that we get bossed around and told we're better off in the kitchen. Write about how we're expected to just make babies and keep our heads down while we're taken for granted.

"Men don't understand how important we are. They don't understand that mothers give their bodies for their babies. They give their lives for their babies. We're expected to keep making all the sacrifices to make everything in life work. But as soon as something goes wrong, we're the ones who get blamed. How can you blame someone who isn't even allowed to voice an opinion?

"For God's sake, we aren't even allowed to vote. Write about that!"

Barb is stunned and wide-eyed. She feels like a tornado has just swept her up. They lock eyes and both stand quietly. Neither knows what's next.

"That's it. You're right, Sally! That is what I should write about, and I plan to do just that!" Barb says confidently, before turning away to go back to her room.

Surprised at Barb's response, Sally steps out from her room.

"Really? Do you think you can?"

Barb stops, turns, and faces her.

"Well, Mr. Darling asked me to write a column that women will enjoy. I just hope women born and raised in Salem, such as yourself, will think the same way that I do. That *we* do."

"I'll be tickled to see it, but I don't think you can pull it off." Sally's tone is friendly... but daring.

"Oh, don't be a doubter, Sally, I'm tougher than I look," she says, popping her eyebrows up and flashing a grin.

Sally laughs. "I can't wait to read it. That's *if* you can get it published in the newspaper."

Barb smiles again. "Just leave that to me."

A few days later, Barb makes her F&D writing debut.

<u>Miss Barb</u>
I Need Your Help
by Barbara McFadden

Hello Ladies!

I'm Barbara McFadden and I'm beyond grateful and excited to be writing to you. I am honored to have been selected for this project and feel like it's fate that brought me here to write this new weekly column for the Farm and Dairy *newspaper. I want to first thank Mr. Darling for the opportunity to reach out to all women in the area. I hope that through this column we can connect to help each other make meaningful progress in our lives.*

I hope to highlight the challenges and rewards of raising a family on the farm, as well as all that we do as women to contribute in a positive way to our community. Each week, I also plan to include a bible verse or two to share, verses that I have pulled strength from.

I have found it very inspiring to see women so active locally and I will do my best to convey the thoughts and feelings of you all, but I will certainly need your help! I grew up on a small family farm, but surely don't have the same experiences that you all do. I invite you to send me any ideas and opinions that you have. You can mail or drop them off at the Farm & Dairy office at 185 East State Street, Salem, Ohio. I look forward to hearing from you!

• *Proverbs 31:26*
"She openeth her mouth with wisdom; and in her tongue is the law of kindness."

• *1 Timothy 3:11*
"Even so must their wives be grave, not slanderers, sober, faithful in all things."

Chapter 6

BARB WALKS INTO THE *Farm & Dairy* office, carrying pressed shirts from another trip to Ray's.

Dee is talking on the phone, but greets her with a smile and a hand gesture indicating she has something to tell her. Barb pauses while she attempts to gather dozens of phone messages. When the other line starts ringing, Dee sets the messages down and waves for help. Dee grabs the second phone and hands it directly to Barb.

"Hello, *Farm & Dairy*," Barb answers.

"Hello, this is Mollie Wiggins with the Salem Grange. I just wanted to call in and say, on behalf of our ladies' group, that we are incredibly happy to see the new column written by Miss McFadden."

"Well, thank you!" Barb replies, gleaming.

"Please let Mr. Darling and Miss McFadden know that we can't wait to see what she will write next."

"Yes ma'am, I will let them both know!" she says with pride.

She hangs up the phone while turning to see a matching grin on Dee's face.

"The phone has been ringing off the hook for you!" Dee proclaims, as she hands her dozens of messages.

Looking at the notes, Barb says, "I can't believe it."

Dee's phone rings again and she scoops it up. "Hello, *Farm*... Why, yes sir. I'll send her right up." Dee flashes another smile at her.

Barb takes a breath, exhales, and smiles back. Then she heads up the stairs.

She approaches the large door at the end of the hall. She takes another deep breath then knocks on the half-open door while leaning in.

"Ahah! Barb, did you hear? They love it!" Mr. Darling bellowed.

She stepped in and couldn't hold back her wide smile.

"Yes sir, I did."

"This is just great. I knew they would love it. Do you know what your next column is going to be about?"

"Well, I do have another idea, but I'm not sure you'll like it. It may be too political."

"Well, I've always believed that politics and the issues of the day are important. And, since you definitely have the ladies' attention..."

He paused and rubbed his chin before adding, "But mind you, try not to get too partisan."

"Yes, sir. Thank you, Mr. Darling."

Chapter 7

Although Matthew Newman is staying at an older motel, he generally likes what he sees of Salem. Once at work, his walk to get lunch downtown is a short, manageable one. But if he's running behind in the morning, the distance between the motel and the hospital is too far.

During the war, working on code ciphers, he was cooped up indoors for twelve or more hours a day. The work was tedious and extremely stressful. Knowing that thousands of lives depended on his being able to decrypt enemy codes was a constant pressure he felt, with little relief.

Walking in Salem is a pleasant, relaxing experience for him.

Working for Dr. Carr is still a challenge, but in a much better way. The kind of way that allows Matt to immerse himself into and enjoy his work. That he can also get outside to grab a burger and fries at his new favorite place, Heggy's, is a welcomed bonus. The corner diner serves up the "World Famous" Heggy's Doubly Cheesy Burger. *Maybe it really is world famous*, he thought after enjoying his first one.

Heggy's is also well-known for having the "Freshest and Best Candies and Nuts East of the Mississippi!" – so says a second sign in their front window. Near the center of downtown, it's a good spot to grab a quick lunch, while also watching the hustle and bustle of State Street.

Staring out the diner's front window – about halfway through his burger and a quarter of the way through a daydream – Matt's attention takes focus.

"Who is that?" he whispers to himself.

A young woman with light brown, curled hair passes by on the sidewalk. Nicely dressed. Not anyone he recognizes.

She's beautiful. I wonder where she's from.

Matt moves to the edge of his counter stool to follow her as she walks farther away. Nearly outside his semi-seated view, she enters a storefront door where the window reads, RAY'S CLEANERS.

How do I meet a girl like her?

"Geez, don't break your neck, kid," the waitress chirps at Matt.

He pops up from his stool and in an instant, without calculation, he pulls a bill from his wallet and slaps it down on the counter. In his hurry, his hand finds the mustard jar, splashing a bright-yellow line of condiment onto his blue tie.

"I've gotta run, Meg!" he says as he heads for the door.

With one hand he holds his tie and then runs his thumb through the wide line of mustard.

"Do you want your change?" Meg calls to him.

"Keep it!" he shouts, with a pointed wave through the window as the door closes behind him. He turns and jumps off the curb to cross the street.

HONK!!!

Tires screech on the brick-paved street.

Matt's hands meet the hood of an abruptly stopping car, as an older man yells from behind the wheel, "What are you, blind? Pay attention!"

Stunned, Matt dumbly nods and steps into the other lane, where yet another stopped driver glares at him.

"Sorry," Matt says, raising both hands in a guilty gesture.

For someone so highly intelligent in the field of mathematics, he's currently losing in the field of common sense. After the cars pass, he walks quickly to catch up with her. He bursts into Ray's Cleaners.

"Oh my!" gasps a woman, as the door he pushes hits her elbow, causing her to drop the cleaned clothes she is carrying.

"I am so sorry," he says, now feeling unraveled. He immediately kneels down to pick up her garments. He helps return them into the woman's arms.

Dumbfounded, embarrassed and ashamed, Matt realizes... it's her.

"Nice necktie," she notes.

He fumbles at what he should say. "You're welcome. Thank you."

"Hey buddy! Were you born in a barn?" It's Ray asking.

Realizing that he left the door wide open, he turns to quickly push it closed.

Turning back to the woman, he begins, "What I meant to say was– "

"I know what you meant to say," she replies.

"Those are very nice suits you have," he says, nodding to the clothes that are back in her arms.

"They aren't mine."

"Well, your husband has great taste."

"I'm not married."

"Oh, then your boyfriend?" he self-corrects.

"No, I don't have a boyfriend." She seems to be enjoying his line of questioning and gives him an encouraging smile.

"So, is that a custom design there?" she points, revisiting his necktie.

Matt looks down with an awkward loss of words. He then remembers the real reason he's at the cleaners.

"Right! It's mustard. I've got to get this tie cleaned." He laughs, shaking his head.

She laughs too, with an affirming nod.

Ray, who has been listening all the while, comes out from behind the counter with a half-dozen ties draped over his arm.

"I have some nice loaner neckties. You can pick one for only five cents," he says in his best salesman's voice.

The woman points to a navy-blue tie with white stripes.

"I think this one would look good on you," she confidently suggests, as Matt unknots his stained tie.

"Thank you, sir," Matt says, turning to Ray. He hands his tie to him in return for the navy one with the white stripes.

The door swings shut behind Matt. He turns and sees the woman giving him a last gaze through the storefront window.

Turning back to Ray, he asks, "Who is she?"

"First, you owe me five cents."

Chapter 8

"PLEASE HAVE A SEAT Lieutenant Groves. I have been looking forward to speaking with someone from the agency," Dr. Carr explains, as he moves around his desk to sit in his chair.

"I have made great progress over the last five years," he adds.

"Yes, Dr. Carr. That is why I am here," says Lt. Groves.

"Of course. Of course. I am sure folks have been wondering all about what I have been working on and the progress. My blood test discoveries, which I will provide you, have led me to follow up with additional studies focusing on the placenta. I know there are many answers to questions we will find in the chemicals within the chromosomes.

"That's if we can assign values to these building blocks within the cells and combine them with other signals. We will have to form an equation from which we can derive a score that I believe will directly correlate to infant death syndrome. With the key information input into the right equation, we will know within hours after their births, which babies are at grave risk. Before there are any visible signs of danger!"

"But, still, isn't all of it just an educated guess?" Groves responds.

"No, no. Not a guess. Let me show you." He quickly grabs a blank sheet of paper from his desk and hands it to Groves.

"Write down any whole number. Do not show it to me."

Groves scribbles a number, without thought.

"Now multiply that number by two."

He does and looks up at Dr. Carr for his next instruction.

"Now add six."

"Alright."

"Take half of your total."

"Okay."

"Now the last one, I want you to subtract your original number."

"Done." The lieutenant looks at him and shrugs. "So?"

"You could have chosen any number you wanted. Any number at all. But I guarantee your final number is three. It was always going to be three," Dr. Carr explains.

"Yes, it's three. But I didn't come here for a simple math trick."

"The point isn't that it's a trick, the point is that you can find an answer that is constant even when using a random variable. I believe through science and technology we can plug our independent variables into an equation with dependent variables to form a linear relationship between the two."

"So, it's not a guess. Doctor, you're saying it's more of a prediction?"

"Yes, sir. I believe it will be an accurate prediction. I just don't have the mathematical skills to arrive at the final equation. "That's why I need Matt."

Groves scowls at him, unimpressed and clearly shows his lack of appreciation for the matter.

"This is life or death! Please. Please allow me to continue this important work. One more year, I'm close. I'm that close, I know it," he pleads.

"Dr. Carr, I have no doubt that your work is important. I know you have done many important things. I am not questioning your work, but what I am here to do is determine if the money we are putting into this project is in the greatest interest of our country's defense.

"There is a strategic shift happening. Now that the Great War is over, we must focus on preventing the next war, or preparing for it. Tens of millions of people died in the war. Developing technologies could make the next war a hundred times worse. Babies won't matter if there isn't anyone alive to make them, Dr. Carr."

"Mr. Groves, I understand what you are saying, but work like this cannot just come to a stop."

"Maybe that's true. But the funding can't come through DARPA any longer. Our priorities are moving elsewhere," he says, standing up. "Doctor, this meeting is to inform you that our funding will stop at the end of next month."

He extends his arm to shake hands as a parting gesture of respect.

But Dr. Carr sits frozen, shocked and in disbelief. Staring aimlessly, he misses the attempted handshake.

"We will collect all of your files at that time, as well," Groves adds.

"No! No sir, you will not! Only half of my files are part of the funded project!"

"Doctor, you know you've been funded through agency grants that make your project classified. All research you have been involved with – and in any manner related to the project – makes it classified, government property," he sternly explains.

"Lieutenant, the notes in the files are coded. There are only two people who know how to read them. If you take these files from me, they will be worthless to you."

"That's fine. Matt can explain to us how to read them."

"Matt doesn't know the cipher. Only Sally and I know it."

"Who is Sally?"

"Sally is my nurse assistant. She's just a young girl, she's very trustworthy and loyal."

"Does she have clearance to read and handle classified material?" demands Groves.

Dr. Carr hesitates before answering.

"Sir, she doesn't even understand what half of it means. I trust her unequivocally. In fact, I delivered her when she was born."

"None of that is relevant. There are no exceptions to the rules. We're done discussing this." He turns and walks out of the office.

Groves leaves the hospital and briskly crosses the street to enter the drug store. Once inside, he locates a phone booth and pulls shut its folding door. He dials a number he knows well.

"We have a problem."

Chapter 9

KNOCK KNOCK KNOCK KNOCK KNOCK...
She rapidly raps on Barb's door.

"Hey, it's me. Sally. Are you in there?"

"Yes, just a second," Barb answers just before opening the door.

"Is everything okay, Sally?"

"Everything is great. I saw your first column, not bad," she judges.

"It's a start," Barb says with a smile. "Please come in."

"I may have been a little bit of a witch the last time we talked. I think I was too tired from work," Sally apologetically explains.

"No, that's all right. I know you work a lot. Do you hate it?" she asks, as they sit on the side of her bed.

"No. To be honest, I really do love it. It's just that I pour all of myself into it, and usually don't have much energy and patience for anything else."

"What all do you do at the hospital?"

"I help Dr. Carr deliver all of the babies. I also help run different tests, record results, and take care of the newborns in any way that I can. Dr. Carr is one of the best doctors and is doing so much that helps make babies healthier. Our infant mortality rates have been cut in half over the last six years. So it just really feels good to be working there."

"Oh my, you certainly do a lot. Is Dr. Carr nice?"

"He is, but he does get a little mad sometimes if I don't keep up with all of his files. I have to go down to his office and file and re-file so many patient files that it sometimes drives me nuts. I guess that's why he's giving me a vacation," she adds proudly.

"That's why I'm bothering you. Do you have a suitcase I can borrow?"

"Yes, I have a small one." She gets up and opens her closet near the bed.

She pulls out her empty half-plaid half-leather bag and tosses it to her. "Catch!"

Sally easily catches it then holds the bag by its leather handles that straddle the top zipper.

"This will work perfect."

"Where are you headed?"

"Niagara Falls. This is my first vacation. Ever! I'm really excited. I'll be attending a conference for nurses and doctors all about infant death syndrome. I bet when I get back, I'll be able to help with the babies even more. I might even learn something that Dr. Carr doesn't know!" she says adding a chuckle.

"I'm so happy for you, Sally. You deserve some time off."

"Thanks. I'm also hoping to get in touch with a friend of mine who I sort of grew up with.

Last I heard she lived near there. I think Buffalo is near there. Anyway, if we can get together, it will be quite a trip!"

Outside of Barb's still-open door, they notice Mr. Lofland in the hall, approaching with his metal toolbox in hand.

"What did you break now?" Sally loudly pokes.

"I just need to tighten Barb's doorknob a little," he replies, standing at her doorway.

"Hi, Mr. Lofland. Thank you for coming so quickly," Barb interjects as she moves closer to examine the problem knob.

"See Sally, that's how to speak in a nice manner to someone," he says sarcastically. He sets his toolbox down and searches in it for the correct screwdriver.

"Luckily for you, you won't have to put up with me next week, because I'm going on a vacation."

Sally starts back across the hall to her room, with the borrowed travel bag.

He calls to her, "That's nice, just make sure you're back here by the first."

"Why, what's on the first?"

"That's when your rent is due!"

They all share a good laugh.

Chapter 10

"EXCUSE ME, SIR," MATT calls out to get the attention of the gray-haired man working on the Lofland House sign.

The old man slowly stands up from his kneeling position, holding a paintbrush in his hand and a small can of red paint in the other. Before speaking, he looks Matt over carefully.

"You know, downtown last week, I almost hit someone with my car. He looked a lot like you look," Mr. Lofland says, while raising his eyebrows with a knowing grin.

"Um, yeah... Well, he must have been a good-looking guy," responds Matt, with a similar grin.

"Ha, that's a good one! I'm Mr. Lofland and I own this beautiful lady. Or more like the old house owns me," he humorously adds. "I'd shake your hand but mine are kind of messy from painting. So now, how can I help you, young man?"

"Well, sir. I walk by here every day, and I've always admired how beautiful your home is. My name is Matt, by the way. Anyway, I noticed the No Vacancy sign is gone, so I figured I better stop and ask."

"I took the sign down, but it's just because I'm touching up the paint on it." He then gestures toward the peak of the house with a point of his paintbrush. "The third floor is the men's floor and I only have three rooms up there, including mine, so there just isn't a lot of turnover... I must not be charging high enough rent!" he says, half-kidding.

Matt smiles along, not entirely sure if he should.

"I recently started working at the hospital, so it would be nice to get a little closer to town," he explains. "I work with Dr. Carr."

"I know Doc Carr. He came to the orphanage to take care of the children a lot. Pretty much everybody in town knows Doc. I tell you what I can do. If I get a vacant room and you're still looking, I'll consider you the first in line for it! Was it Matt?"

"Yes, sir. Matt Newman. And thank you, sir." He pulls a scrap of paper from a pocket and scribbles his name and phone number on it. He hands the slip of paper to him. "It's been nice to meet you, Mr. Lofland."

"You can call me Keith. Now remember, I won't put the Vacancy sign up 'til I get in touch with you first."

"Thank you again, Mr. Lofland. I mean Keith. Enjoy your Saturday." He turns and heads back to the sidewalk and continues his walk into town.

Through her open window, Barb initially heard, then watched the two men talking. Peeking through the drapes – not wanting to be seen eavesdropping – her view wasn't very good. She thought she recognized the stranger's voice from the dry cleaner. She decides to make it a point to bring it up when Mr. Lofland sets out dinner later.

"Spaghetti here, meatballs in this dish. If you need more sauce, it's on the range," a hungry Mr. Lofland announces, as he grabs his own plate to fill.

"Who was that man talking with you out front today?"

"He said his name was Matt Newman, and that he works at the hospital with Doc Carr. Coincidence that I almost hit the young fella with my car last week!"

"What did he want?"

"He wanted to see if we had a room available, he's probably tired of the roach coach he's staying in and wants something nicer and closer to town," he explains.

Barb nods while twirling some pasta onto her fork.

"Why, do you know him?" he asks, as the meatball on his fork falls off and lands on his lap. "Darn it!"

"I think I met him once. Informally."

"You know, I'll bet Sally knows him. She works with Doc. We can ask her when she gets back."

Chapter 11

"WELCOME TO THE NIAGARA Falls of Canada, the honeymoon capital of the world!" the train conductor bellows.

Sally had never felt so privileged in her life. Just riding the rail to the Falls, she thinks, self-mocking as she gazes out the passenger car window that partly reflects her excited smile. She had never left Salem before. Her emotions have her feeling giddy and nervous at the same time.

She wants to hate her nervousness, but she can't help knowing that this is the most exhilarated she has ever felt in her life. It's as if she had never really lived until now.

"Sir, can you please tell me the way to the Clifton Grand Hotel?" she politely asks the conductor.

"Yes, of course. Once you step off the train, the first street on your right will be Clifton Hill – take that until you can turn right again, then just walk toward the mist of the Falls. The Clifton Grand Hotel will be on your left. You can't miss it. If you're in the water, you went just a bit too far," he jokes.

Sally is so focused on understanding his directions, it's a few moments before she gets it and laughs along with him.

"Thank you very much."

Once she turns onto Clifton Hill she is awestruck. The power and beauty of the Falls spellbind her. The sound of the rushing, crushing water calm and humble her.

"Wow," she softly utters. It's like nothing she has ever even imagined.

She walks toward what she thinks must be a lavish government building of some sort. White columns stand all along the stone building, supporting an extended roof that stretches over the balconies on its highest floors. She continues on and stops at the corner of Clifton Hill and River Road, still enamored by the mist and sound from the

Falls. She looks back at the stately building that occupies the corner. Two, painted white, brick pillars stand in front of it, one with a brass plaque that displays, The Clifton Grand Hotel.

Sally stands in the entrance rotunda of the hotel.

It's bigger than all of downtown Salem! she thinks. She can't believe it, taking in the busy scene. To her left, she could see the green felt of several pool tables in a billiard room. To her right, she could see a gentlemen's smoking room and a bar. Rounding the rotunda are smaller rooms identified as Telegraph Office, Ticket Office, Information Bureau, Gift Shoppe, and Guest Study. She approaches the long reception desk.

"Welcome to the Clifton Grand Hotel," greets the man behind the desk.

"I just can't believe this place," Sally says, still admiring everything.

"Thank you. We are quite proud," the middle-aged gentleman replies. "Have you never visited here before?"

"No, sir. This is my first time."

"Well, she burned to the ground twenty years ago. Rebuilt in oh-five to be even bigger and better! We have two dining rooms, a café and a handful of tearooms. Each of our 270 guest rooms has electric heat and lights, as well as hot and cold running water," he boasts.

"Well, ain't that honey!" Sally replies in uncontrolled amazement.

"Are you staying with us?"

"Yes. I'm here for the medical conference."

"Very good, those meetings will be held in the Palm Ballroom. I think you will find it quite accommodating as well, Miss... ?" he enquires while reaching for a long drawer full of small cards.

"Sally, Sally Kimins."

"Ah yes," he says, plucking her card from the drawer. "You will be staying in room 421. You will have an excellent view of the Falls!"

"Oh, my! This is wonderful," she says, amazed more by it all. "May I ask, is it possible for me to place a telephone call?"

"Of course, Miss Kimins! Your room comes with a modern rotary-dial telephone, so you may call as desired," he touts. "Plus, all calls made within the Niagara Falls-Buffalo area are considered local and don't require operator assistance or additional charges. We just had these new rotary-dial telephones installed. Our guests love them!"

Sally's eyes open almost as wide as her smile. This feels like a dream. A bellhop takes her borrowed travel bag and escorts her to her room.

She grew up in the orphanage with a girl who was like a sister to her. After the orphanage closed, Sally and Violet wrote letters and cards back and forth a few times a year. In a recent card, Violet wrote that she had gotten a job at the new post office in Buffalo.

Sally hopes she can reach her by telephone. There's only one way to find out. After referring to the directory in her room, she dials the only listed number for a post office in Buffalo.

"Hello, is this the Buffalo Post Office?"

"Yes, ma'am, it is. How may I help you?" asks the cordial but efficient male voice.

"And is this the *new* post office?"

"Yes! Built less than a year ago. We're the newest, most modern post office in Buffalo," he proudly adds. "Now is there some way I may help you, ma'am?"

"Does Violet Daniels work there?"

"Yes, but today is her day off. May I take a message?"

"Oh, yes! Please tell her that Sally Kimins – that's me – is at the Clifton Grand Hotel until Monday."

Chapter 12

<u>Miss Barb</u>
Our Time is Now!
by Barbara McFadden

Dear Ladies,

Thank you all so much! I believe it was my fate to write this column, and your positive and uplifting responses are proof of that. Thank you all again! I had no idea this many letters would be sent in – 184, to be exact! Knowing so many strong women are reading the Farm & Dairy *and my column, I'm feeling more passionate than ever.*

Though I do not yet know mos
of Salem's history, I was insp..
to find out that one of the first
women's rights conventions ever,
was held here in 1850. One of
the topics at that convention was
women's suffrage. Unfortunately,
we are to this date, still unable to
vote. As women, we have not been
legally recognized as "equals." But
every day we prove ourselves as
such.

We may not have been created
to do everything a man can do,
but humanity relies upon us to
do what a man cannot. It was
written into law nearly 50 years
ago that all men had the right to
vote. It is way beyond our time
to be afforded the same right and
privilege! A democracy cannot be
"of the people, by the people,
for the people" without all of its
people having their say. Voting is
our say, and I say that our time is
now!

The National American Woman Suffrage Association will be sponsoring a petition table at Salem's upcoming Jubilee Festival. In addition, petitions will be circulating downtown. I hope you all have a chance to sign it. I'm confident our perseverance will soon be rewarded!

• Proverbs 31:11
"The heart of her husband doth safely trust in her, so that he shall have no need of spoil."

• Psalm 46:5
"God is in the midst of her; she shall not be moved: God shall help her, and that be right early."

—❖—

BARB ARRIVES AT WORK a little extra early. She wants to be there actively working before Mr. Darling arrives. He was out of town early in the week and had not reviewed her second column before it went to press. She's afraid she might have pushed it too far to the edge. She isn't sure what Mr. Darling will think.

"Did you read my column?" Barb asks Dee, who's sitting at the reception desk.

"Yes. I liked it, and we have gotten some calls. You also got some more mail. And we have sold out all of the copies we have in house as well!" she notes.

"Has anyone been upset at all?"

"I wouldn't say so. I've had a couple complainers. But my pen went dry, and I didn't get to write those down," Dee says with a forgetful tone, shrugging and smiling.

Just then, Mr. Darling makes his entrance. Dee jumps from behind the desk to receive his jacket and hat.

"Good morning, Dee."

"Good morning, sir. How was your trip?"

"Very good, it went well. I love the big city," he adds.

"This morning, your wife called to say she will be dropping by." Dee looks up at the office clock and adds, "In a few minutes, actually."

"Uh oh, did I forget something? Or am I in trouble?" he says with a smile. Then he turns his attention to Barb.

"How is Miss Barb, this morning?"

"Just fine, sir," Barb replies, still a bit nervous about what might come next.

"Dee, do you have any other messages for me?"

"Yes, I do. Quite a few. Lynn from Butler Grange, Martha from the bank, Helen from the shoe store– "

"Oh, the ladies are after me today," he jokes. "Just hand me the stack."

After being away, he knows he's behind and has some catching up to do.

"Oh, and Dee, do you have my copy from this week's print?"

"Yes, sir. I had to hide this one because we ran out," she says, handing him the folded paper.

"Well, that's a good sign. They always seem to sell better when I'm not around. Ha, I guess I need to take more vacations!"

He chuckles as he heads toward the stairs to his office. Paper in one hand, briefcase in the other. Just then, Mrs. Darling gusts in through the door, stopping him in his tracks.

She's pretty yet looks tough. Her demeanor is elegantly aggressive. Dressed to the nines, she's sharp, clean and pressed. Her jewelry is showy. Gold-clad diamond earrings. A gold brooch with a carved face in white stone. And a gold necklace drapes from her neck, featuring a golden charm dangling at its bottom.

"Did you see the paper, Wayne?"

"I've got it right here."

"Did you approve this?" she asks, pointing to a specific column in her copy.

A confused Mr. Darling, not sure if he's answering for something good or bad, replies with a confident guess. "Course! Course I did."

"I'm not sure if I believe that," Mrs. Darling says, amused. But anyway, the ladies at breakfast were extremely excited about it."

Barb sits silently, wondering if this is about her latest column.

"That's swell, I'm glad they're interested in what we're doing." He's still not sure what his wife is referencing.

"I want to meet this *Miss Barb*," his wife demands.

"Well, she's right there," he nods.

Barb quickly stands to attention.

"It's genuinely nice to meet you, Miss McFadden. I really like what you are doing," Mrs. Darling praises.

"Thank you, Mrs. Darling. It's nice to meet you, too," Barb says, with plenty of hidden relief.

"If he gives you any trouble, you come straight to me," she says, turning to flash a look and a wink her husband's way.

"Yes, Mrs. Darling," Barb quietly replies with a smile.

Mr. Darling starts up the stairs. "Aw, I knew I was in trouble!" he says playfully.

"Keep up the excellent work, Barb," she reiterates.

"Yes, ma'am. I will do my best, Mrs. Darling!"

Chapter 13

SALLY HAS SOME FREE time away from the
conference to explore Niagara Falls, but
decides first that she'll buy some postcards.
She has always loved the idea of receiving a
postcard from some far-off place. She's even
more excited to be able to send one to thank
Dr. Carr.

Maybe I should send one to Barb, too.

She takes the elevator to the lobby and
goes to the front desk, where she gets the
attention of the man who checked her in.

"Hello. Do you sell postcards and postage?"

"Why yes we do! Let me have our concierge
escort you to our Gift Shoppe. We have
a fine selection of postcards and stamps
there. Once you are ready to mail your

cards, just bring them right back here and place them in this outgoing tray. Feel free to use one of our writing rooms or the café to fill them out."

"I think I will. Thank you!"

"Oh, before you go, you're Miss Kimins in room 421, correct?"

"Yes, I am."

"We received a telegram for you this morning. Just a moment... Here it is."

"Oh, thank you," she says, surprised. A new level of excitement shows on her face, as she reads the telegram:

11:00 AM Sunday.
– Brunch.
– Your hotel restaurant.
– Regrets only.
– Your friend, Violet

Chapter 14

BARB STROLLS ALONG THE sidewalk and opens the corner door of Heggy's. She walks in and sees a familiar person eating at the lunch counter.

"Oh, I know you," she says as she approaches the nearby candy counter.

"But do you really?" Matt teases, smiling at his quick wit.

She smiles back before answering, "I know your name. It's Matt Newman."

"So, you found out my name. Then it's only fair that you tell me yours," he says, still smiling. "Are you eating lunch here?"

"No, I'm just in to get some candy. I find that no one cares how long of a break you take as long as you return with treats," she jokes.

"May I help you?" politely interrupts a young man wearing a tag officially identifying him as Confectioner.

"Excuse me, Mr. Newman," she says, turning away to answer. "Why yes, thank you. I'll have a half pound of mixed nuts and a half pound of your assorted milk chocolates, please."

They watch him begin filling the order. After adding, then subtracting, then adding morsels again into a box on the scale, he appears exasperated. He finally asks, "Will a little *over* a half-pound of chocolates be alright with you, ma'am?"

"That'll be just fine. Thank you for asking."

He puts the small box of chocolates into a pink bag, and then puts a yellow bag on the scale.

Next, they watch him have more difficulty weighing the nuts. He scoops, weighs, subtracts, drops some, and again adds too many. Barb and Matt look at each other, not saying a word. She decides to rescue the confused confectioner.

"I've changed my mind. I'll take more of those nuts, too, if you don't mind."

He removes the bag from the scale, looking relieved. Then he grabs his pencil and notepad to total the amounts.

"Okay then, with the tax, this is ninety-five cents exactly," the high-school teen says shyly.

Unaware his weighing processes were witnessed, he takes care to point out, "This pink bag contains your box of chocolates, ma'am, and this yellow bag has the nuts." He places them upon the glass display. "Here you are."

"And here you are. Please keep the nickel."

"Wow, thanks. And thank you for your business, ma'am. Please come again!"

"I certainly will!"

She takes the bags and looks over at Matt.

"Mr. Newman, my name is easy to find out. You could just read my column in the latest issue of the *Farm & Dairy*. Oh, I'm sorry. I just remembered it's sold out this week."

Certain she got in the last tease, she turns to leave.

"It's even easier if you just tell me," he suggests as she walks out the door.

From the sidewalk, Barb turns with a confused look. Her hand cups her ear, as she didn't fully hear him. She mouths "What?" Then she shrugs, as if not caring what he said anyway, as a devious smile crosses her face. She waves and heads across the street to where Matt first saw her from the spot in the diner where he always sits.

She heads back to work, to the writing she has to start and finish. Her third column's deadline is this afternoon. But she's still not sure what to write about. She gets back to the newspaper and pulls the nice box of chocolates from its bag and places it on the front desk. She pours some of the nuts into a small dish on the reception desk.

She decides to move her typewriter out of the open reception area to a side office to try to gain better focus. She balances the typewriter on her hip so she can grab a handful of chocolates on the way.

Neither the nuts or candies are helping her get started. She's blocked. The blank sheet of paper stares back at her. Another chocolate's crunched-up wrapper joins the pile on the desk.

Should I follow up my last column with something more mundane, more everyday? Or should I continue to push the envelope? If I don't, am I letting other women down? Will I lose the momentum that I've built for the column?

Out of boredom and frustration, she raises the nearest window shade. Her thoughts continue racing as she gazes out the window.

People watching, hmm. Who's going where? Why? What brings us here? What's our purpose?

Her thoughts are interrupted. A young woman is pushing a baby stroller with one hand, while holding her toddler's hand with the other.

That's it!

<u>Miss Barb</u>
Mother's Work
by Barbara McFadden

Dear Ladies,

I've enjoyed reading your many messages, cards and letters. Thank you for educating me more in the ways of life around these parts.

Many of you who read the Farm & Dairy were born on the land that your families have always farmed. The hospital is the birthplace for most of the rest of us.

Whether it was in a stable, in an old farmhouse or into the hands of Doctor Carr, we were all brought into this world from our mother's womb.

A child is born and in what seems like an instant, a daughter becomes a mother – a new life begins and hers is changed forever. Motherhood is a gift both given and received.

What a beautiful and important relationship. Some of us are blessed to have more time with our mothers than others but, still, we all share this intimate connection.

A young mother who was making her way down the sidewalk with two children – she inspires my column today. I'm sure she had errands to run that brought them downtown. But a mother's responsibilities aren't limited to when the errands begin. She must get both an infant and a toddler cleaned up, fed, dressed, and gathered up, all while doing the same for herself.

Once in town, she must, hopefully keep her children happy, under control and out of harm's way. While pursuing what she needs to get done in a day. As hard as it is, most mothers handle tasks like these endlessly, while somehow making it look easy.

I am not a mother yet, but I do pray that someday I will share the joys and responsibilities of motherhood.

President Woodrow Wilson designated the second Sunday in May as Mother's Day, making it a national holiday. But I believe mothers should be celebrated every day. To all of you with the strength and courage to do a mother's work daily, I celebrate you and yours.

• Ezekiel 16:44

"Behold, every one that useth proverbs shall use this proverb against thee, saying, As is the mother, so is her daughter."

Chapter 15

SALLY SITS IN THE Palm Ballroom listening to the final speaker of the conference. She's sad to see the conference come to an end, but she also looks forward to getting back home. She took detailed notes on each presentation and can't wait to apply some of the new information and ideas. Her careful notes on the latest research methods will certainly interest Dr. Carr.

She always knew there was life outside of Salem, but it was almost a "had to see it to believe it" experience for her. It was still a surreal feeling to sit in such a large and lavish place, getting to see so many new and exciting things and to have it all paid for through work, no less.

"Have you enjoyed the conference?" A voice from behind her asks.

Unsure if the question is directed her way, Sally turns slowly. Over her right shoulder, stands a man looking at her, waiting to hear her answer.

"Um, yes sir. I have."

"Sir?!" he says with a smile. "Please, just call me Rob."

Sally eyes his name tag. Dr. Robert Brock

She gives him a quick once over. His dark hair is neatly cut and combed. He's sharply dressed, like you would expect a younger doctor to be. Crisp pleated khaki pants, a light blue dress shirt and a navy sport coat. No tie, which seems surprisingly unprofessional. But it is the last day of the conference, after all, she thinks. His brown dress shoes didn't have laces, but instead gold buckles. Very sharp.

"You look too young to be a doctor."

"Ha, thanks! It's a blessing and a curse I suppose. Sometimes I can feel patients wondering if I'm old enough to deliver their babies."

"Oh, you're an obstetrician. I'm a nurse for an obstetrician!" she enthusiastically shares.

"Well, how about that!" he replies. "Say, are you going to the cocktail party tonight?"

"No, I... I can't."

"Oh, you're heading out of town already?"

"No, I just can't. I'm meeting a friend tomorrow morning."

"Okay then, let me buy you just one drink," he pleads, then smiles.

She's a little nervous. She would love to have a drink with the good-looking doctor, but she isn't 21. If she gets carded, it would be too embarrassing.

"I would love to, but the truth is, I'm not 21 until tomorrow," Sally confesses.

"Wow! You're as young as I look!" Rob jokes. "So tomorrow, Sunday, is your birthday?"

"Yep, the 31st."

"Well then, you'll be legal at midnight! You have to let me buy you a drink for your birthday!"

"Midnight, huh?" she ponders out loud, realizing he's right.

"Yes, at the bar just around this corner?" He points out a conference room door.

"Okay, I will see you there at midnight... Rob!"

"Great, uh..." He peeks around her to read her name tag. "Sally. Yes, I'm looking forward to being the first person to toast you on your birthday, Sally!"

As they temporarily part ways, they smile at the idea of seeing each other later.

Chapter 16

AFTER RUNNING WEEKEND ERRANDS around town, Barb heads back to the Lofland House. It's a beautiful day with a light breeze under a warm sun, so she takes the slightly longer route through the park.

As she approaches the kitchen door at the rear of the house, she smells dinner cooking. Once inside, she can hear Mr. Lofland setting the table.

Entering the dining room, she compliments, "Something smells wonderful!"

"Yes and thank you. It's an old family favorite of mine."

"Oh? What is it?"

"It's part of a couple surprises I have planned for dinner tonight," he teases.

"Just what I want, surprise food," Barb kids him back.

"I think you'll like it. If not, then that's just more for me," he quips.

While admiring the lacy tablecloth she'd never seen before, she notices something else is different and asks, "You've put down an extra place setting. Has Sally returned from her conference already?"

"No, she should get back tomorrow, so she can pay her rent on time!"

"Then why the extra plate?"

"I told you there would be surprises," he says as he places silverware around the table.

"Okay, keep your secrets." She pretends to sigh. "I'll go get cleaned up. See you at six."

"Don't be late!"

As Barb gets seated in her favorite place at the table, Mr. Lofland fills the water glasses. She can't help but be curious about tonight's dinner guest.

"Is one of the other residents coming down to eat with us tonight? I rarely ever see them."

"Well, the others are either too old to want to go up and down the steps, so I take them a plate. Or they don't want to be social," he explains. "Either way, I've always respected them. And they pay on time. But that there plate is part of one of my surprises."

"Oh, that's bologna!" Barb says with a laugh. "You're just pulling my leg!"

"Maybe a little," he says with a wink. Then he walks through the swing door into the kitchen. A minute later, he comes back carrying a cast iron pot.

"What's that? One of your surprises?" she prods him for answers.

"This is just the gravy."

"It's now after six, you know. Your surprise is late. You better ring your dinner bell."

"Go ahead, you can ring it," he says, heading back into the kitchen.

Barb takes it as a dare and leaves her seat to give him a little surprise of her own.

Ding-a-ling! Ding-a-ling! She rattles the bell with great vigor, then quickly returns to her seat.

Mr. Lofland backs his way through the door, this time carrying a serving plate full of toast. He nods toward her, as if to say he's impressed with her bell-ringing ability.

"Toast??" she asks, bemused.

"Can't get anything past you, now can I?" he playfully mocks.

He puts the plate down on the table, just as he notices Matt walking from the foyer into the adjacent living room. Barb's back is toward him, so she doesn't see him entering the dining room.

Mr. Lofland looks up and barks, "You're late!"

She whips her head around to see who the dinner guest is. She knows Matt. What the heck is going on? She wonders and quickly turns back to the table.

Matt sees her and is more stunned than she is. It takes him a few seconds, yet all he can say is, "I know. I'm late. I'm sorry, Mr. Lofland."

"Barb, this is our new tenant, Mr. Matt Newman. He's moving into old man Hippley's room. Hippley's daughter felt he was too old to live on his own. I had to agree with her. Have this seat here, Matt," he says, pulling out the chair across from Barb.

"We've met," she says, as Matt takes his designated seat.

"Good, get more acquainted. I just have to grab another thing," he says, heading back to the kitchen.

"Barb. So that's it. I finally know your name," he says with an accomplished smile.

"So then, I guess you didn't read my column."

"Uhm..."

Before Matt can think of an excuse, their landlord bursts back through the door with a large plate of dried beef.

"Surprise, Shit on a Shingle! That's what we used to call it. Tear a couple pieces of that toast up on your plate, then do the same for this beef. Then you pour the gravy over the top of it all. Dried beef and gravy over toast. It's pretty good stuff!

"Then, my last surprise is dessert! I have a minced meat pie if you have room for it later," he proudly adds.

Everything for dinner on the table, he makes up a plate and is about to leave them.

"Please excuse me, I have to run this plate up to my other third floor tenant."

After he disappears up the steps, Matt breaks the ice.

"I didn't know you lived here. Do you like it?"

"I do like it. Mr. Lofland does a wonderful job with the place. That is, as long as he isn't trying to burn it down." She adds lightheartedly.

"What?"

"He told me the other day he accidentally caught the front porch on fire."

"He seems like quite the character."

"Yes, he can be a lot of fun. And Sally is quite the character, too. Don't you work with her?"

"Yeah, I do. Sally lives here, also?

"She does and we've become rather good friends. She seemed a little rough around the edges when I first met her, right here in this room. Since then, I've come to know that she has a heart of pure gold. And a passion for her work with Dr. Carr."

"Really? I don't see her that much at the hospital, but she always seems to be taking care of some task or another. I know Dr. Carr really appreciates her. He has mentioned that he really likes her assisting with the newborn babies."

"Probably because they can't talk back to her and tick her off! Seriously, Mr. Lofland seems to have a special place for her in his heart, too."

"That's good to hear. By the way, how's your Shit on a Shingle?"

"It actually tastes better than I imagined it would."

"I agree, it certainly tastes better than it looks."

"And much better than its name sounds!" adds Barb.

They share the humor, then a bit more silence. But now the silence seems comfortable to them.

"Well, I think I'm going to pass on the minced meat pie," she says, and picks up her empty plate.

"It was nice to officially meet you, Barb," he says, as she stands to take her dish away.

"Yes. Officially!"

She looks at his shirt, slightly smiles, then asks, "Matt, is that gravy on your tie?"

He looks down and sees that his tie is... perfectly clean.

They both laugh, as she heads toward the swinging door.

"Good one, you got me, Barb!"

Chapter 17

MATT TAPS ON THE pebbled glass of Dr. Carr's office door.

"Come in."

"Doctor, I've been working and reworking the formula and order of operations, and I think I'm onto something. At least, I'm getting numbers that correlate to risks for the newborns. When I do the calculations, I come up with what I am calling *risk scores* -- so far, the scores range from two to more than 34,000."

"That's an awfully wide range, Matt. I think we need to be able to have an assessment with a range of... let's say, one to a hundred, or to a thousand."

"I agree. But let me explain the connection I found within my first data set. From the first four files, I've pulled scores, to the nearest tenth, of 2.2, 5.7, 84.1, and 34,277.0. They were from the Frederick, Lough, Kindler, and D'Angelo files, in that order."

"Okay, now one at a time, what were the scores again?"

"Frederick, 2.2."

"Marian Frederick?" asks the doctor.

"Yes."

"She was born five weeks premature. Poor thing never had much of a chance," he recalls.

"Next, David Lough had a score of 5.7."

"What's the chart say? Pyloric stenosis? We tried to correct it, but it was too late."

"Then, Charles Kindler was 84.1."

"This was recent. Crib death… I'm not sure if these are making sense, Matt."

"Nicholas D'Angelo, score of 34,277.0."

"I know this family well, and I don't think they've had any issues at all. Nicholas should be 10 years old by now."

"Exactly. When the risk score is high, I'm finding there are no health issues in early development. When the score has been under a hundred, there are major issues. I think if we can calculate these risk scores right after birth, we'll have a much better chance of assessing and correcting an issue before it's too late."

"Matt, we need a greater sample size. Keep calculating files and when you get to your 40th, we'll re-examine the data. In the next batch, start with the Kimins and Newburn files, plus the Daniels file. They're all from the beginning of my study and I know those files best."

"Yes, sir."

"This does show promise. Well done, Matt! It could help to show Groves something new like this. I had better call and let them know we're making significant progress. So, get me the data on the next set as soon as you can."

"Right away, Dr. Carr."

Chapter 18

THE MINUTES ARE PASSING slowly. Feeling anxious but excited, Sally sits on the edge of her hotel bed. She has never been in this situation before. She dated and went to dances when she was in high school, but the last few years she has socially been a hermit – only going between work and the Lofland House. She isn't sure if she should go down to the bar a little early, a little late, or try to time it to get there right at midnight.

"Ahhhh..." she groans. She falls back onto the pillow, thinking too much, and it's frustrating.

"That's it!" She pops up from her bed.

I'm going to be early. Waiting around and thinking about it is worse than just going down.

The elevator dings and the door opens. "Ground floor, please," she says to the operator.

What happens if he's not there? The thought crosses her mind as she exits the elevator to walk down the hallway toward the rotunda.

If he isn't there, I'm leaving. But I'm early. Should I just sit at the bar and wait? I'll just go back to my room, but then the elevator operator will think I'm crazy. No, I'll take the stairs back.

As she enters the bar, her thoughts are racing.

"Sally! You made it!"

Oh god, he's here.

Rob is at the corner of the bar and has saved a seat for Sally, between his and the wall. He gets up and greets her with a gentle hug and a jubilant greeting. "Happy Birthday!"

"Not quite yet, I don't think," she jokes, as she shimmies onto the tall bar-stool.

"Close enough in my book! What can I get you to drink?"

"Uhm, I'm not sure."

"Well, what do you like? Oh, right! How could you know!" Rob laughs.

She nervously laughs with a shrug of embarrassment.

"Take a sip of this. It's called an Old Fashioned, it's made with bourbon."

She holds the glass and takes a small sip. Her tight-lipped swallow is followed by a scrunch of her nose and a forced smile.

"Okay, we'll have to try something else." He does his best not to laugh again.

Sally smiles off the new, unwelcome taste of bourbon.

Rob turns to the barkeeper. "Hey Burt, how 'bout a Bees Knees for the lady?" Then he turns his attention back to Sally.

"So, you said you work with an obstetrician? What do you do?"

"I'm a nurse. I help with whatever is needed."

"What do you like best about it?"

"I like being able to help mothers and their new babies."

"So, do you help with the testing and measurements, or are you just in the nursery?"

"I share all of those duties, but I'm the only nurse who does Dr. Carr's paperwork and filing. The other nurses only handle the hospital's paperwork."

The barkeeper sets her drink down with a napkin in front of her.

"Thanks, Burt. Her drinks are on me."

He turns in anticipation of watching Sally try her new drink. She takes a small, careful sip of her Bees Knees, and then licks her lips.

"Much better!" she exclaims.

"Oh good, it's a sweeter drink, gin and honey," he explains. "So, where are you from?"

"Salem, Ohio."

"Never heard of it, but I don't know Ohio well at all," he admits. "I'm from Brooklyn. Have you ever been to New York City?"

"No, I haven't. This is actually my first time out of Ohio."

"Well, you did it right! You probably passed through two other states and made it into a new country, all in one trip!" he praises. "New York is great. I bet you'd like it."

"Yeah, I'd like to see it someday!"

"You said something about doing separate paperwork for your doctor. What did you mean by that?"

"Oh, well, Dr. Carr is a top researcher in infant care. He studies babies and their blood and he works to cure birth diseases. Some of his work is so important that we have to use numbers and codes in our files. So nobody else can read them."

"Codes, huh? That's quite interesting."

"Yeah, Dr. Carr's very private about his research. But he needed help, so he taught me how to code our research files. He trusts me!" she boasts.

"It looks like you enjoy that drink. I need to go to the washroom. I'll be right back, okay?"

He stands up from his stool and waves to the barkeeper. "We'll have two more drinks down here, Burt."

"So, you liked that last drink, miss?" the bartender asks.

"Yes, you make very tasty... what are they, again?"

"Bees Knees."

"Yes, tasty Bees Knees."

"Thank you."

Thoughts about a bustling New York City start flashing in her head, as she has more sips. She has never seen more than a couple pictures of *America's City*.

I wonder what it would be like. It must be as busy as this hotel rotunda at midday.

Being that it's late, the bar has mostly cleared out. Sally still can't believe the week she has had.

For years, it's been nothing but working away the days at the hospital. And now, look at me. I've traveled to a different country and I'm having cocktails in a swanky bar.

A more confident smile crosses her face. Just then, Rob returns to his stool and sees her expression.

"Looks like you're glad to see me!"

"Who, *who* are you?" she kids.

"I'm your Prince Charming. And you're my Cinderella. But only after midnight!"

They laugh at the magical comparison.

"I think those drinks are getting to you, my dearest Cinderella."

"Oh, but I feel fantastic!" she admits, then giggles as she tosses her hands up.

"Exactly!" he says. "I have to be careful with you, because you know how to write in secret codes!"

"Yeah, you *better* be careful!"

"Are you so good that you can teach me how to work with secret codes?"

"I'm that good. But I don't know if you're *smart* enough for me to teach you," she challenges.

"Oh! You got me there. You're pretty sharp. For a nurse."

Sally raises her hand, as if to slap him. "Don't make me." She tries to keep a straight face but can't.

"You're funny. Seriously, I really like you, Sally."

"I like you too, Rob," she says, looking into the cute doctor's eyes.

Time stands still for several breathless seconds.

Then, he leans in for a kiss. She meets him halfway. The simple peck only lasts a moment. Both pause and are silent, still only a couple inches apart. Their eyes meet again, as if they're sharing the very same thought... *What will happen next?*

Sally leans back to take an excited, deep breath.

"I *do* have a few files up in my room. If you want to learn how secret codes work, I could show you."

Chapter 19

As it rings, the phone seems to shake on Dr. Carr's desk.

"Hello, this is Dr. Carr."

"Hello Doctor, this is Lieutenant Groves. I was told you have an urgent message for me."

"Yes, we have made a new discovery. Matt has found a formula that gives us what I call a *risk score* that very accurately shows us which children are at early risk for major health issues. I truly believe this is a breakthrough for modern, medical science."

"That's fantastic. You solved your math problem, and you did it with weeks to spare."

"Yes, so I was hoping that since we're making such significant progress that we could discuss continuing and, perhaps, adding to our project's funding."

"Well Doc, you accomplished your goal. I'm sure you're proud of yourself. But as I said when we met, we're making the change so we can focus our budget on the defense of our country. And by the way, I'm having all of the project's research files picked up sooner. This Monday morning."

With that, Groves hangs up.

Chapter 20

As Rob escorts her to the elevator, Sally has an arm wrapped around him.

"Doctor. Dr. Brock!" someone shouts across the hotel rotunda.

"Excuse me for a second, Sally," Rob says.

He turns to see a man quickly walking in their direction. He clearly recognizes him and walks to meet him about 20 feet away from Sally.

"I'll get the elevator," says Sally, who is now only a few strides from it.

A few moments later, the elevator dings. She turns around to see Rob coming back. She yells, "Okay, Mr. Popular, better hurry or I'm leaving without you!" She laughs.

He quickly catches up to the elevator and steps in, turning to close the cage door behind them. Sally pushes the fourth-floor button.

"Who is that?"

"Just a colleague of mine," he answers, while still facing the elevator door. His attitude seems to have changed, and his new silence fills the elevator.

"So. We will see if Dr. Popular is smart enough to learn a code!" She smiles at him.

"I'll do my best, Sally."

The elevator stops and he opens the cage for her. As they start down the hall, she takes Rob's hand and leads him to her room.

"It really is pretty simple, the vowels are numbered, as well as the letters J and R. The rest of the alphabet is just folded back on itself to represent another letter. We used to have a chart until I got it memorized. Cuz I'm smart."

As they make their way to 421, she hands her room key to him.

"I feel light, I feel happy!" she chimes, as he holds open the door for her.

"That's called *drunk*," he says good-naturedly and definitely amused.

As he flips on the wall switch, Sally dances past him into the room. She turns on the desk lamp, then takes two files from her bag. She drops the folders on the bed and takes a pencil to write ROBERT on a piece of hotel stationery. Below his name, she slowly writes, 73N57G.

"This is your name in code," she says. She holds up the paper to show him.

"Are you supposed to have these files?"

"Dr. Carr let me make copies of my file and my twin sister's file. I was the very first baby born that was part of his research study. But my sister and mother both died. Right after I was born."

The room goes quiet.

"But it's okay, Rob... I don't remember them."

A minute passes before he says anything.

"Sally, I must tell you something. I work for DARPA."

"I don't understand. Dar...?"

"I work for the agency that funds Dr. Carr's research. My bosses were very unhappy to find out that he allowed you to handle classified information. It's illegal. Let alone the fact that you have removed classified material and have it with you now."

"Illegal? I just help Dr. Carr."

"He is going to lose his funding, and probably his medical license because of this."

"Oh, no, no, please. You can't, I don't want to hurt Dr. Carr!"

Sally's eyes begin watering. She's angry, she's hurt, she's reluctant. She stands up aggressively.

"I did nothing wrong! I will just quit. You can take my files."

"Sally, I'm sorry. I'm sure he is going to be disappointed, but there isn't anything I can do. I'm supposed to watch over you tonight and you will be arrested in the morning."

She sobs and pleads through her tears, "This isn't fair. I didn't know. Please Rob, you have to help me."

He pulls out a paper from his jacket pocket.

"Here, write a note to Dr. Carr and I'll make sure he gets it. Tell him you're very sorry and that you never meant to disappoint him. Also, by writing this, you will show remorse, and I can try to change my superior's mind in the morning."

She throws the paper down on the bed, and begins gasping for air, trying to hold back more tears. Finally, pulling herself together, she picks up the paper and writes.

Dr. Carr, I am so sorry.
I did not mean to let you down.
Love, Sally

"I'm sorry Sally, but for you to have these government files and to be telling someone you hardly know about the code is a terrible situation. Not to mention being drunk. It looks terribly bad."

She slumps onto the foot of the bed, shaking.

"Isn't there anything you can do to help me, Rob?" She's begging.

He sits down beside her and wraps his arm around her.

"I'll try my best to help. Actually, I do have some pills you can take so you aren't drunk in the morning."

He pulls two pills from another pocket.

"All of this will look better if you aren't hung over. Let me get you some water."

He comes back from the bathroom with a small glass of water.

"Here you go, Sally."

She puts the pills in her mouth and drinks them down.

"It will be okay," he assures her.

"This is all my fault." Her head droops. Her tears fall to the floor.

"Sally, I think we can make this all go away. I know you didn't do this on purpose."

He stands next to her and takes the water glass from her hand.

"We'll figure this all out in the morning. You just need to get some sleep."

She turns over on the bed and crawls to the top, plopping her head down onto the pillow.

"Here Sally, take two more. I want to make sure you don't have a hangover in the morning."

She turns back and raises herself to take the pills. He hands back the half-filled glass and she washes them down. She falls back into her pillow, still crying.

"I'll be right here," he says calmly, as he collects the paper she coded on, her apology note and the two folders. He places the note and water glass on the corner of the bedside table. Next, he pulls out a handful of the same pills. He slowly lets them drop from his hand across the table — a few roll off and fall to the floor.

"I'll take your phone off the hook, so no one disturbs you," he says. He carefully places the receiver on the table.

He turns back to the bed and puts his hand on Sally's shoulder. He gives her a shake and asks, "Are you awake?"

She doesn't respond. He shakes her harder. Still no response. He turns to leave her room.

Should I turn off the light?

He thinks through possible scenarios and decides he should leave it on. At the door, he stops and turns for one last look at her.

I'm sorry it has to end like this. I really got to liking you, Sally.

Chapter 21

THE BRASS DOORKNOCKER JUMPS and rattles after each pounding of Dr. Carr's fist on the door. Impatient, he pounds five more times. He stands on his toes to peek through the door's beveled glass panes. A figure is approaching the door, so he steps back.

Mr. Lofland opens the door.

"Doc, hel– "

"Is Matt here?" he interrupts. He's soaked from the down-pouring rain.

"Sorry for the wait, Doc. I was headed up to the attic. I have to check my roof repair for any leaks. Matt's in… " He finishes the sentence to himself as the doctor rushes past him. " …the dining room."

When he sees Matt sitting at the dining table, he nearly shouts, "It, it's days, Matt!"

Matt turns, surprised to see him. "Dr. Carr, is everything alright?"

"No, no it's not," he answers, entering the room. Then he stops, stunned, not expecting someone else would be in the room. Barb is also sitting at the table.

"I need to speak with you, Matt." He adds, "Privately."

Matt stands up. "Yes, sir."

The doctor's intensity has everyone worried. Matt leads him through the swing door into the pantry room off the kitchen.

Curious, Barb follows but stops at the door as it swings back, closing.

Dr. Carr passes Matt into the kitchen, looking around to see if it's secure enough for his liking. Without anyone in sight, he can no longer hold back what is pressing him. He turns to Matt, and the focused look on his face forecasts a moment of significant importance.

"The risk score, your score. It's *days*," he says in a powerful whisper.

Matt shakes his head then whispers back, "I don't understand."

"The number is days, Matt... Days."

He's still confused.

Starting to relax enough to better explain, Dr. Carr continues.

"The equation you created, that gives us a score. I've been reviewing the files. Your scores are equal to days. The number of days that someone will live, Matt."

"No, it just correlates a risk based on our data," he replies.

"Matt, you now have almost a hundred files calculated. The scores were so accurate, I started seeing a pattern. It's so accurate, it's been correct in every single death!"

"So then, what do the high scores mean?"

"It means they have longer to live."

Matt stands dumbfounded. He can't believe it. He steps forward and puts his hands upon Dr. Carr's shoulders.

"It can't be true. We can't predict when someone will die."

"We can now, Matt."

They realize the house phone in the kitchen has been ringing.

"Welcome to the Clifton Grand Hotel!"

"Yes, thank you. I'm here to meet someone for brunch," Violet says while looking around the hotel's rotunda for Sally.

"Our Sunday brunch is immensely popular, the maître d' can get you seated. Just through those doors there," the man at the front desk says, pointing to his right.

"Thank you."

"Good morning, miss! Do you have a reservation? We are quite busy today," the maître d' says.

"If we do, I assume it would be under the name Sally Kimins. We weren't to meet 'til eleven o'clock. She may not be down yet."

He looks down and moves his finger along the reservations list.

"Here it is. I see your table is ready. Would you like us to ring her room to let her know you're here?"

"Yes, thank you very much."

He seats Violet at their reserved table, where a waiter pours water into both crystal glasses.

"Would you like some orange juice or coffee?"

"Orange juice, please."

"Why, of course."

Fifteen minutes pass before the waiter returns.

"Another glass of orange juice, miss?"

"Yes, and may I ask you a favor?"

"Certainly."

"I am to meet my friend Sally Kimins who is staying here. She may have celebrated her birthday last night, so she could very well be *under the weather* this morning," she says, followed by a sly smile.

"Ah, the weekend flu," he replies, with an understanding wink.

"They were to ring her room, but she may not have heard it. Could you ask the maître d' to try again, or send someone to knock on her door?"

"Yes, of course"

Another half-hour passes by.

Finally, the maître d' comes to the table.

"Miss, could you please come with me?"

She must have drunk herself silly last night, Violet thinks, as she pushes back from the table. "Of course."

They walk toward the front desk where the hotel manager instructs the maître d', "Seat her in my office, please."

"Yes, sir," her escort responds.

"Is everything okay?" she asks.

"I'm sorry, I really don't know. But I'm sure someone will be right with you to explain."

He then leaves her in the office, closing the door behind him. Several minutes pass before a man, who appears to be wearing his Sunday best, opens the door and enters.

"Hello, I am Detective Reiter of the Niagara Parks Police Service."

"Is something wrong?"

"I first must ask you a few questions. What is your name, miss?"

"Violet Daniels."

"You're here to meet Sally Kimins?"

"Yes. Is she okay?"

"Were you with her last night?"

"No. We only planned to meet today for brunch."

"When did you last speak to Miss Kimins?"

"I haven't *seen* her in years. Over the last couple of days, we exchanged messages about getting together here at the hotel. Her birthday is today. I don't understand what's going on."

"Do you know her family and how we may contact them?"

"Sally is an orphan. She has no family. Detective, has something happened to her?"

"Well, Miss Daniels, the phone calls you asked the hotel to make to her room didn't go through, so they sent a bellhop to her room. When his repeated knocks went unanswered, he was authorized to let himself in. Unfortunately, he found your friend in bed and unresponsive. The manager and hotel doctor went to her room, then called us immediately."

"Is she okay? Where is she now?"

"I'm sorry, Miss Daniels. It appears to have been a suicide."

"What? How?!?"

"The evidence shows she was drinking, and it appears that she took too many sleeping pills."

"No, that can't possibly be!" Tears begin welling up in Violet's eyes.

"I should let you know. She left a suicide note. I am very sorry, Miss Daniels."

He pauses until she composes herself.

"Please leave your home or work telephone number. I can call you if we get any additional information. Here is my calling card. You're free to leave the hotel now. Again, I'm sorry about your friend."

"Can somebody pick up that darn phone?" Mr. Lofland yells from another room. "I need to go to the attic to make sure the roof isn't leaking!"

Dr. Carr and Matt pause, looking at each other. Frustrated at the interruptions, the doctor pushes the pantry door open and walks to the kitchen phone.

"Lofland House."

"Hello, this is Detective Reiter. I'm calling about Sally Kimins."

"Sally isn't here," he curtly replies. Then he hangs up the phone.

"Okay, Matt. We need to get to the hospital."

As they head for the back door, the phone rings again. More annoyed, Dr. Carr quickly picks it up.

"Hello."

"This is Detective Reiter of the Niagara Parks Police Service. I need to speak with someone about Sally Kimins."

The doctor finally focuses on something else. "A detective? What's this about?"

"Yes, sir. This is the telephone number Sally had listed when she checked in at the Clifton Grand Hotel."

"Okay?"

"We've been told that Sally has no known family. Are you able to confirm this?"

"Yes, Sally was an orphaned child. What is this regarding? Is she in some kind of trouble?"

"Miss Kimins was found dead in her hotel room this morning. She died from an overdose of sleeping pills mixed with alcohol, and she left a suicide note. Even if she has no family, we feel we need to inform someone who knew her."

Dr. Carr is shocked. His rote subconscious takes over to push out the words, "Thank you for letting us know, Detective."

He hangs up the phone and stares in disbelief at Matt, who's waiting for some kind of clarification.

"Sally killed herself."

Matt's jaw drops and another wave of confusion crosses his face.

Barb bursts through the kitchen door. "WHAT DID YOU SAY?"

All he can do is blankly and slowly repeat, "Sally killed herself."

"How can this be?" Barb asks. She turns to Matt for an answer, any answer. But none comes.

"They're wrong. We need to investigate this," she says in denial.

"Doctor Carr," Matt says sternly, trying to pull him out of his trance-like state. Then it occurs to him. "You delivered Sally. We have her birth file. If what you were saying before is correct, we can reference her risk number to double check."

He looks up at Matt, takes a deep breath and then turns his attention to Barb.

"How long were you listening to us?"

"Long enough."

"Both of you, listen to me. We cannot mention Sally's death to anyone, especially Mr. Lofland. You absolutely must trust me on this. I will explain everything later. But right now, we've got to get to the hospital!

"I'll leave a note for Keith," he adds.

Matt walks into Dr. Carr's lab office holding the file folder he retrieved from the research files. He sits down at the worktable and reviews his calculations. To be certain, he goes over them a second and a third time. Then he announces, "Sally's risk score is 7,670.29."

He drops the open file on the desk. Next, he walks over to the chalkboard where he begins dividing Sally's risk score by 365.25.

Dr. Carr and Barb watch anxiously as he chalks through the process to produce the number 2 near the top of the board. More writing below and another result above. This time, it's a 1. He finishes his calculations then adds a decimal point followed by a string of digits, 0-0-0-1.

Matt pronounces, "The final result is 21.0001." Astonished, he looks at Dr. Carr who is shaking his head, confirming their fears.

"But what does that result mean, Matt?" asks Barb.

"The risk score in Sally's file was 7,670.29. Dr. Carr hypothesized that the score represented a total number of days. So, I divided that score by 365.25 – the number of days in a year – to give us this final result of 21.0001 years."

Dr. Carr elaborates, "Sally was born 7,670 days ago. Today is her 21st birthday which, according to our calculations, matches up with the day she was fated to die."

"What do you mean by fated?" she asks.

"I collected information from Sally, her mother and their shared placenta within hours of her birth. Once that information was placed into the equation Matt created, it gave us her risk score. We thought that a low score simply showed an elevated risk for newborns. But now we know that the score represents the exact number of days that a baby will live. From the day she was born, we could have known the day she was going to die. From Sally's birth to her fate date. Today."

"Oh, my god." After a silent pause, she asks, "So you can know when anyone will die?"

"No, not exactly. Matt's equation uses specific information that can only be collected and recorded soon after birth. You would have to have someone's results from those tests, certain information about their mother, and results from specific tests run on the placenta. All of that data needs to plug into the equation."

"This is crackers," she says, overwhelmed by what she's hearing.

"Nobody else can ever know what we know," the doctor warns sternly. "You can never speak another word of this to anyone. But before we leave, we need to destroy all of the birth files. We absolutely must get rid of them. Tonight."

Chapter 22

IT'S MONDAY MORNING AND Dr. Carr sits at his desk, beaten down and exhausted. Over the last twelve hours he has been ravaged by emotions. His work was his life, but he knows they had to destroy every file. Nearly 40 years of research reduced to ashes in a hospital dumpster.

Worse than that, Sally is gone. He doesn't want to accept it, it's just too much. He's miserable.

By mid-morning, Matt returns to the hospital. He and Barb had finished helping destroy the doctor's files only a few hours ago. Before returning, he had been hoping that DARPA would show up the very first thing this morning. He was hoping to miss their formal questioning and blame regarding the missing files. As his head is spinning, the receptionist at the front desk hails him down.

"Good morning, Matt. I have a bundle of mail for Dr. Carr. Would you mind taking it down to his office?"

"Oh, good morning. Of course. Has anyone been in to see him yet this morning?"

"Nope. No patients, no visitors so far."

Darn it, he thinks. "Thank you," he says. Taking the mail, he heads to the stairs.

Dr. Carr is resting his head on folded arms when Matt knocks on his door, unintentionally waking him.

"Oh, I'm sorry to wake you, doctor. It was a long night. I have your mail here."

He places the rubber-banded batch on his desk.

"I've been thinking, Matt." he starts slowly. "It might be better if you aren't here when DARPA arrives."

Thank God.

"There's no reason you should take any blame for any part of this. I'll tell them that I alone destroyed the files. And I won't mention anything about our discovery. Let Groves be angry with me. He'll be just as happy that he doesn't have to fund my research."

Matt sees that the weight of the entire situation and the impending DARPA issues are wearing on him. But there's nothing more he can do and, to be honest, he's relieved that the doctor wants him to leave.

"Okay. Maybe I'll go downtown for an early lunch." Wanting to help without thinking first, he continues, "Do you want me to bring something back for you to eat?"

"No, I'm not hungry. You need to go now. But thank you, Matt."

After Matt leaves his office, a piece of colorful mail in the bundle catches his eye. He works the rubber bands off and pulls out a card.

It's a picture postcard from Niagara Falls.

He flips it over to see if there's anything
written on it.

Dr. Carr,

*I hope you receive this before I
return. It has been a great trip.
The falls are breath taking! You're
the closest thing I've had to a
father, and I just wanted to thank
you for all the help you have
given me. I'm excited to apply
some things I have learned during
the conference. Thank you for
everything!*

Love,
Sally

It breaks him. As he convulses and cries, he
drops his head again onto his desk.

Hours have passed. The telephone rings and wakes Dr. Carr. He sniffles, wipes his eyes then clears his throat before answering.

"This is Dr. Carr."

"Hello Doc, Lt. Groves. I want to let you know my boys are heading over to pick up our files. I want to congratulate you again on your breakthrough and wish you luck as you move forward."

Silence.

"Doc, you there?"

Dr. Carr was worried about what Groves would say after finding out the files were destroyed. But now, he just doesn't care. There's nothing left that Groves can take from him. He erupts, shouting into the phone.

"YOU WILL NOT GET A SINGLE FILE, LIEUTENANT!"

"I don't think you under– "

"No. *You* don't understand! I told you before and I will say it again, it's my life's work and research files and I can do with them as I damn please. I never agreed to turn anything over to you. And I don't think anyone should know when they're going to die. It's not what I ever intended!"

A longer silence.

"Calm down. Take it easy, Doc. What exactly do you mean about knowing when somebody will die?"

Carr takes a deep breath. He realizes his mistake.

"Dr. Carr, what did you mean by that?"

"I burned all the files. They're gone. Every single one of them is gone. So, I guess it doesn't matter if I tell you or not... If you were born today, I could tell you with 100% certainty, the day you will die, your *Fate Date*."

"Are you serious?"

"Yes. It's why I had to destroy the files. *Nobody* should ever have that kind of information."

"Dr. Carr, that's for us to decide. But if you can prove your findings and give us a blueprint to replicate them, I'll make sure you get your funding back. This could be extremely useful information for us to have. And you can have your life back."

"No, sir. I am done."

"But what you're forgetting is that I know that Matt knows the formula."

"The formula's worthless without those patient files. He plugged in the research data, but the rest of each file detailing where the data was from, the rest of it was coded."

"Ha, ha! Of course, you're so smart," he mocks. "Doc, before I go, I want you to know... I have retrieved the duplicate files from Sally."

Click.

Chapter 23

BARB IS SITTING AT her desk. She's expected to have a new column turned in by the end of the day. After last night at the hospital, she can't focus enough to think about writing. Everything from the kitchen phone call to the dumpster burning continues running through her head. Last night was horrible. This morning the nightmare won't let go of her.

She hasn't mentioned Sally's death to anyone. Partly because she wishes it's not true, and because away from the boarding house and the hospital, nobody else knows or would care about Sally.

The bell on the front door jingles, pulling her from her daze. It's Mr. Darling. She quickly reacts by sitting up in her chair and showing an attentive smile.

"Good morning, Dee," he says in a blustery voice. "Good morning, Miss Barb."

She feels pressure to look busy, but she can't fake it.

"Good morning, Mr. Darling," she responds, in as upbeat a manner as she can muster.

Mr. Darling and Dee begin a conversation about their weekends, and the messages she has for him. Barb's focus fades again.

"Miss Barb. Miss Barb?" Mr. Darling is working to get her attention.

She snaps out of it to realize he's now speaking to her. "Um, yes?"

"You will have a new column for us this afternoon, correct?"

"Yes, sir. I was just running it through my mind."

"Very good. I look forward to it." He turns and heads up to his office.

She exhales a deep breath of frustration. It's as if her body feels stress and is trying to reset itself. She's not worried about writing the next column, but the events of the last 24 hours are proving a stressful distraction.

"You're quiet this morning. Is everything okay?" Dee asks.

"I'm fine," she answers, not sounding so fine.

"Maybe you could take a quick walk and get some fresh air. Sound good to you?"

"Yes, I think I will. Thanks."

Relieved by Dee's suggestion, she stands up from her desk. As she heads to the door, she sees a familiar face through the window. It's Mr. Lofland.

He enters through the door she was about to open.

"Hello, Dee."

"Hi, Keith. How are you?"

"I'm doing fine. How about you?"

"Doing well. What brings you in?"

"I want to make sure this lady gets the postcard that came for her in today's mail."

He extends the card to Barb, making sure to look at her directly. His eyes seem to deliver some kind of confusing message to her. Or maybe she's imagining that he knows something she knows. Regardless, her curiosity is piqued – yet cautious – as she accepts the postcard from him.

"Thank you," she says. Her full focus turns to the card.

Mr. Lofland probably said something else, and the bells on the door probably made their usual sounds as he left. But she's going back to her desk and doesn't hear anything.

Her eyes devour the unexpected mail. Her heart is beating out of her chest. She reads the card once, then again, and again.

Barb,

This trip has been amazing. The waterfall is so strong and powerful, just like us! For the first time ever in my life I feel like things are looking up. I feel so independent and free. I look forward to telling you all about it when I get back. Thanks again for letting me borrow your bag!

Your friend,
Sally

P.S. There are a lot of cute doctors here!

Barb had intuitively known that something about Sally's suicide didn't feel right. Now, she has no doubts. Sally didn't kill herself.

Inspiration is an understatement. She knows what she'll do next. She rolls a blank sheet of paper into her typewriter and begins. Fifteen minutes later, she hands her column to Dee.

"Well, that was pretty quick!"

"I'm going to take that walk now. If Mr. Darling is looking for me, just be sure he gets my column."

"I'll definitely make sure he gets it, Barb."

Chapter 24

<u>Miss Barb</u>
Every Day is a Gift
by Barbara McFadden

Dear Ladies,

Do you ever wish you could have done things differently? Have you felt cheated, or like life just isn't fair? Unsure what to do next?

Recently, I lost a close friend of mine, and it has made me re-evaluate what is most important to me. Perspective has been hard for me to find.

A person close to me is gone

*and that has made me feel all
kinds of emotions. I will admit,
I first felt sad but began to feel
angry. Something made me feel
like I needed to blame someone
or something for her being gone.
Rational thoughts finally allowed
me to see the light.*

*Obviously, I know there is nothing
I can do to bring her back. I
can only try to be as thankful as
possible for the friend that she was
to me. God works in mysterious
ways...*

*Ultimately, I want to remind
myself, and anyone else going
through something similar, to
hold the fond memories close
to your heart and focus on the
positives. Every day is a gift and
an opportunity to cherish those in
our lives.*

*Sally Kimins will always remain
an important person to me.*

All of us have important people who shape our lives, and we are also important people to others. No one can do everything on his or her own. Daily, we rely on so many others in our community to play their roles in society.

Help someone today. Enjoy the little things in life. Leave your worries behind. Pray for others and appreciate every second you have with your loved ones!

- *Psalm 133:1*
"Behold, how good and how pleasant it is for brethren to dwell together in unity!"

Chapter 25

MATT IS LEAVING THROUGH the hospital's main lobby when two DARPA agents arrive, looking and walking toward him. He can't hide his anxiety and wishes there was a way to not be noticed. In his haste, he trips on the corner of a floor mat and nearly falls to the floor. He rights himself in front of the agents.

"Matthew Newman?" inquires the taller agent.

"Yes, that's me."

"In the pharmacy across the street there is a pay phone. Lieutenant Groves will call you there at ten hundred hours. That's in ten minutes. Don't miss the call."

"Yes, sir."

He walks outside knowing the agents will soon find out there are no files for them to collect. He wonders before they speak on the phone if Groves knows about the files being destroyed. Either way, he trusts that Dr. Carr will not tell them about his involvement in burning them.

The phone rings on the wall inside the corner booth. Matt answers it. "Hello."

"Hi, is this the pizza place?"

"No, their number ends with 0554."

"The one on Second Street?"

"No, the one on Lundy."

The agency's phone line protocol completed, Groves has confirmed he's speaking with him, Matt waits for the conversation he doesn't want.

"I have to talk with you about your next project. Before I do, I need to know if anything Dr. Carr has discovered would be helpful to national defense?

"I don't think so, sir."

"Did he ever explain to you anything about the codes in the files?"

"No, sir."

"Okay. Newman, you are relieved of your duties at the hospital. I want to see you on a bus headed back to D.C. this afternoon. One more thing. Did the doctor ever mention knowing when people will die?"

Matt nearly choked on his tongue. "Uh, no sir. Nothing. No, he never said anything like that." *This is not good.*

"In that case, I'm going to think about your future some more. For the time being, stay put at the hospital. I'll be in touch with you tomorrow."

Matt feels like Groves didn't believe his answers. He's relieved that he doesn't have to head to D.C., but the last place he wants to go back to is the hospital.

Groves hangs up his phone then slides the bowl of pistachios on his desk closer. He fishes around and finds nothing but empty shells. He checks the cellophane bag they came in. "Empty, damn it," he mutters.

He opens his desk's top drawer and picks out the exact change he'll need. He stands up and walks into his outer office.

"Ruth, I'm going down the hall. Any important calls from above, say I'm in a short meeting and take as much detail as they'll give you. Tell them I'll call back ASAP."

"Of course, Mr. Groves."

Once in the employee lunchroom, he surveys the three vending machines. "Why the hell do they keep changing these things?" he asks no one.

"For once, stop moving them around. How hard is it to keep the cigarettes, snacks, and stamps in the same places? And that goddamn change machine never gives back the right amount. Jesus Christ, I don't have time for shit like this," he announces, again to no one.

After vending more of his favorite snack, he heads for the men's room. All the stalls are empty. He chooses his – the one at the end – and closes its door behind him. He sits down for no reason other than to rip open his new cellophane bag. But he does so with too much force.

His red-dyed pistachios bounce and dance in every direction on the bathroom's polished marble floor.

"Fuck it!" he yells.

Back at his desk — without any nuts or calls from higher-ups to return — he finishes reviewing the department file he had Ruth pull before his call to Salem.

Already frustrated, he looks through the rest of the classified personnel folder. He whispers to the small paper-clipped photograph inside, "So Matthew Newman, you insist you don't know anything? If that's what you want, have it your way. But what am I going do with you?"

Just then, his direct line rings.

"This is Groves."

"Sir, all of Dr. Carr's files are gone."

"Never mind the files. Off the books, I'm changing your assignment." He's now holding the young analyst's photo.

"What we talked about before. Make it two."

Chapter 26

HIS MIND IS MUDDLED. Matt's trying to solve all of his problems at once, but has yet to solve a single one. On top of the Groves issue, if it comes to it, he doesn't want to leave Salem. In truth, he doesn't want to leave Barb.

What am I going to tell her?

"Are you ready to order, or do I have to come back a third time?" the Heggy's waitress wants to know.

"Just a burger and a chocolate shake. Thanks."

"For breakfast? I guess we'll call it brunch," she jokes, as she tears the order slip from her pad and heads to the kitchen.

Matt just nods. His mind is elsewhere. He wishes he was.

He floats through brunch and decides he needs to go back to the hospital to talk with Dr. Carr, to try to get a handle on what Groves knows and doesn't know.

He walks to the hospital and down to Dr. Carr's lab. As he slowly passes the file room, he sees the cabinet drawers open and empty. He rounds the corner and enters the doctor's office, but he doesn't see him. He proceeds to the lab, but still doesn't find him.

"Doc? Are you here?"

No answer.

Maybe he's upstairs.

As he starts down the hall, he glimpses a patch of white behind Dr. Carr's desk. He backtracks to take a second look.

It's Dr. Carr? On the floor?

He rushes into his office.

"Dr. Carr!" he shouts.

The doctor is face down. The back of his lab coat has several red blotches. Blood. Matt quickly but carefully rolls him over.

"Dr. Carr! Dr. Carr!"

He checks him for the slightest breath. He doesn't detect any. Then he checks for a pulse.

He's dead.

Matt begins hyperventilating. He drops to the floor on his hands and knees, fighting to catch his breath. He moves so he can sit up against the wall.

He's panicking. He focuses, yet it still takes him nearly a full minute to regain his normal breathing.

Again, he falls back against the wall. He wants to run and hide, but he's paralyzed with fear. His head feels like it's on a swivel, as he looks around the office for answers, at least clues.

He begins thinking that he may not be alone. His mind flashes back to the DARPA agents he ran into in the lobby.

Did they do this? Could they be coming after me, next? Do they know about Barb?

He needs to leave quickly. He gets to his feet and stands over Dr. Carr's blood-stained body. He sees something stuck to the doctor's coat, reaches down, and removes a postcard.

Could they have? I've got to find Barb!

About to rush out, he has a sudden moment of clarity. He turns, kneels, and reaches into the doctor's pockets. He finds his keys.

He hurries down the hall to the rear door of the basement. He slowly opens it to look outside. He sees nothing unusual in the parking lot. It appears safe, so he walks directly to Dr. Carr's maroon Cadillac. He finds its key on the ring, gets in, then starts the car.

He drives out of the lot and heads toward the *Farm & Dairy*. His only hope is that she's there. As he turns onto State Street, his adrenaline is rushing. He feels hyper-alert.

There she is!

He spots her walking down the sidewalk on the other side of the street. He slams on the brakes.

Matt calls out, "Barb, get in. Hurry!"

Without hesitating, she runs to the car and gets in. He drops the clutch and begins driving.

"What are you doing?!"

"I think they killed Dr. Carr. I think we're in danger!" he says urgently. He picks up the bloodstained postcard.

"Here, take a look at this."

Barb quickly recognizes what it is. From her purse on her lap, she pulls out the card she received from Sally.

"I got one, too. Could somebody have killed both of them?"

Before attempting an answer, Matt turns the car into the Lofland House driveway.

"I don't know. God, I hope not. We should grab a few things that we need to leave town," he says, pulling under the carport.

"If we see Mr. Lofland, don't say anything about this," she says.

They rush to their rooms and are back in the car within minutes. He turns the ignition key.

"I left enough money for both our rents on the dining room table," she says.

"Why?"

"I think the first place they'll look for us is here. If they know we just paid our rents for the month, they'll probably wait here for us to return."

"That's good thinking," he says, impressed but sober.

As they begin pulling out of the driveway, they see Mr. Lofland trimming hedges. He turns to see who's leaving, so Matt slows to a stop.

Recognizing the car, he kids, "Who'd you steal that Caddy from?"

Matt hesitates.

"Dr. Carr let us borrow it for the rest of the day," replies Barb.

"That's sure nice of him."

"It is. Oh, by the way, we put our rents on the dining room table."

"Thanks. Well, you have a nice drive."

"Okay, we'll see you later today," she shouts, to be sure he hears.

He does and can't resist shouting back, "Not if I see you first!"

They snap back to reality and wave their goodbyes to him. Matt drives down the driveway and stops short of the sidewalk. He looks both ways.

"Which way do you think we should go, Barb?"

"West. Turn right and let's drive straight out of Salem."

A few minutes pass, during which Barb closely examines the postcards for any clues they might offer. She wants to figure everything out. But she finds no clues. The cards clearly can't give her answers, but the *one* thing she knows is that Sally's death wasn't an accident. She looks at the road ahead of them, then back at Matt.

"Thank you, Matt," she says calmly.

Their eyes meet.

"I couldn't leave Salem without you, Barb.

"I know."

She smiles warmly at him, then looks out her window. Several silent minutes pass. About two miles out of town, on both sides of the state route, corn stalks stand at attention for as far as one can see. Her eyes glaze over as the cornfields fly by. She's thinking.

What is going on? Where should we go? What should we do?

Barb realizes she's still holding the postcards and focuses her attention back to them. But her thoughts are traveling elsewhere, to the column she just finished writing. She takes a deep breath and slowly exhales, hoping to regain her focus on where they're going. She takes another deep breath before speaking.

"Slow down."

He touches on the brake pedal and responds, "What for? Why here?"

"Just slow down. Slower, slower. There, right there, on the left! Turn there!"

She points to a mostly washed-out gravel access road that runs between two cornfields.

He brakes in time and carefully makes the turn. The Caddy's cushioned suspension handles the rutted road like a large boat moving over small waves. The cornstalks hide the car from the main road's sight lines.

Still confused, Matt asks again, "Why are we here, Barb? Where the heck are we going?"

Perhaps too deep in thought to hear his questions, she says, "For safe keeping, I'll hold onto these."

She slides both postcards into her purse.

As she turns to look into Matt's uncertain eyes, she pulls out a pistol.

"Stop the car."

POST CARD

Pearl,

This trip has been amazing. The waterfall is so strong and powerful, just like us! For the first time ever in my life I feel like things are looking up. I feel so independent and free. I look forward to telling you all about it when I get back. Thanks again for letting me borrow your bag!

Your friend,
Sally

P.S. There are a lot of cute doctors here!

Post Cards of Quality. — The Albertype

THIS SPACE FOR MESSAGE

Eastland House
Attn: Pearl McFadden
566 S. Lincoln
Salem, Oh. 44460

THIS SPACE FOR ADDRESS.

C. 36. On the Canadian Niagara Boulevard, Horseshoe Falls in background, Niagara Falls, Canada

CANADIAN SOUVENIR POST CARD

THIS SPACE FOR CORRESPONDENCE   THIS SPACE FOR ADDRESS ONLY

Dear Carr,
    I hope you recieve this before
I return. This has been a great trip,
the falls are breath-taking!
You're the closest thing I've had
to a father, and I just wanted to
thank you for all the help you have
given me. I'm excited to apply
some things I have learned during
the conference. Thank you for everything!
                        Love, Sally

Attn: Daniel Carr
1995 State Sreet
Salem, Oh. 44460